A SACRIFICE

SWIFT PRESS

First published by Swift Press 2024

First published in Great Britain under the title *Tokyo* by Cargo Publishing 2015

1 3 5 7 9 8 6 4 2

Copyright © Nicholas Hogg 2015

The right of Nicholas Hogg to be identified as the Author of this Work has been asserted in accordance with the Copyright, Designs and Patents Act 1988

Offset by Tetragon, London

Printed and bound in Great Britain by CPI Group (UK) Ltd, Croydon, CR0 4YY

A CIP catalogue record for this book is available from the British Library

ISBN: 978-1-80075-223-8
eISBN: 978-1-80075-224-5

A SACRIFICE

Nicholas Hogg

Swift

Ravens have been recorded swooping over bands of gorillas, teasingly playing at attacking them. These birds show the ability to deceive that comes with the power of language. In this they are no different from humans. Where humans differ from ravens is that they use language to look back on their lives and call up a virtual self.

John Gray

MAZZY LOOKED DOWN onto moonlit clouds. No break in the feather bed cumulus laid out from LA to Tokyo. There had been one shining moment, when a streak of silver glittered on the surface of the sea, like a sheet of worked metal. Then again the cloudscape, the anger at being pulled from a Californian high school to Japan, her father. So she looked to the perfect moon, craters and scars from ancient collisions. Lonely in the thoughts of a lifeless rock, she turned back to the plane and the sleeping passengers. Some comfort in the other bodies.

The Japanese man beside her was in his mid-twenties. Hard to tell with skin that even toned and smooth. He was sleeping. Or his eyes were simply closed. Mazzy would have to wake him to excuse herself past to go to the bathroom. It seemed a shame to disturb his peace, the Buddha-like repose. The faint lines at the corner of his mouth were the only hints of ageing, and the more she looked the more immaculate he seemed to appear. Five hours into a transpacific flight his black shirt was barely creased, and not a strand of his thick dark hair out of place.

Still, she wasn't holding it in across the width of the Pacific.

"Sorry," she said. "Excuse me."

He didn't even seem to be breathing, let alone waking to allow her past. She had to reach over and touch his arm.

He opened his eyes and stared, as if she were some precious creature stepped from his dream.

"I need the bathroom," said Mazzy, pointing down the plane.

Slowly, the man nodded. Though rather to approve some private thought than to acknowledge her presence. Again, she said she had to use the bathroom. This time he smiled and stood, bowing a polite apology as she squeezed out from the seats.

Mazzy walked past the slumbering passengers. Slurred faces

before the glowing screens. She didn't see how he watched her walk the darkened aisle, the way she tied back her long blonde hair. She took her time in the cubicle. Washed her hands and studied her eyes. Her father's daughter, she knew that much. His high, stern, forehead, a serious focus to her resting features. But the wide smile breaking out across her cheeks when needed.

When she got back to her seat the Japanese man was looking out of the window. Sitting in her place. His face almost pressed to the glass. Now she noticed marks under his jaw, a bruise or graze running under his left ear.

Perhaps he saw her reflection, the change of light. He quickly turned and apologised. "Sorry." An American accent to his broken English. "I had to look at the moon."

He shifted over then stepped into the aisle, so Mazzy could move past.

"It's beautiful on the clouds," she said, sliding back to her place.

Before she began the inevitable small talk on who was going where and why, he asked her if she knew the Japanese folk tale about a moon princess.

"A moon princess? I don't think so."

Whether the man took this as an invitation to tell seemed unimportant. He had to tell. He sat straight and erect, spoke.

**

Once upon a time, an old woodcutter was walking through a bamboo forest when he noticed that one of the trunks was glowing. He took his axe and chopped it open to find a baby girl, no bigger than his thumb. He cupped his hands and carried her home to his childless wife. She was overjoyed they now had a daughter to raise.

They named her *Kaguya-hime,* the luminous night princess.

At first the couple tried to keep her a secret, but she grew into such a beautiful woman that five princes proposed to her. *Kaguya-hime* didn't want to marry any of them. She set each one an impossible challenge. The first had to bring back Buddha's begging bowl from India, the second a jewelled branch from a mythical island, the third the robe of the Chinese fire-rat, the fourth a precious stone from a dragon's neck, and the fifth a cowrie born from a swallow.

The earnest men set out on horses and ships. All of her suitors failed. One drowned. When the Japanese Emperor heard of this strange and beautiful woman, he journeyed to the village and also fell in love. *Kaguya-hime* turned him down too. She told the Emperor she couldn't marry a man from the earth, and that she must return to her people on the moon.

The Emperor tried to imprison *Kaguya-hime*, and surrounded her house with guards, but the moon people rode across the stars and blinded the soldiers with a strange light. She told the woodcutter and his wife that although she loved them she had to return to her family. Before the horses galloped into the sky, *Kaguya-hime* wrote the Emperor a letter and gave him a cup of everlasting life.

When he read her last words he broke down and ordered the letter to be burnt. He couldn't live forever without being able to see her again. His men took the letter and the elixir to the top of Mount Fuji and set it on fire.

The legend, when Fuji was still an active volcano, was that the smoke was the eternal burning of the letter and the everlasting life.

**

Narrator and listener. As if they were the only two awake on the plane. When the Japanese man had described an ivory carriage ridden down from the moon, Mazzy had felt the skin on the back of her neck turn cold.

After he finished the story, Mazzy had sat for a moment, pictured the snowcapped peak of a perfect mountain, pale horses in the night sky. Then she told him her name and asked him his.

Instead of answering, he said he was tired, and then folded his arms and closed his eyes. She presumed his insouciance was simply a cultural difference, and put her headphones on and scrolled through the in-flight films.

When the captain announced they were beginning their descent into Narita, Mazzy woke up. The seat beside her was empty. Blanket folded, the headphone wire neatly wrapped. She looked around for the Japanese man, but he must have moved places while she was napping.

Then the plane cut through the clouds and the coastline twinkled with sunlight, a thin line of surf between land and sea.

With the other jet-lagged and flight-stale passengers, Mazzy shuffled towards immigration. Every few metres there was a chirped welcome from a uniformed official. Though she could only guess it was a welcome as her Japanese was not much more than please and thank you. She'd never taken the wrapping from the language textbooks and CDs her father had mailed.

She walked the quiet and empty corridors, like school during lessons when she snuck out of class. The Japanese officials doing the job of hall monitors ready to check your pass, a reason for being where you were. For that she'd have to defer to her father.

Then the booths and fingerprints. Look into the camera. "Can I smile?" she asked, knowing, from the thousands of digital photos that either she or one of her friends had taken, she looked a whole lot better if she dimpled her cheeks and showed an expensive set of gleaming teeth.

Narita was not the bustle of LAX, dogs and guns. Border guards twitchy because half the world wanted to be in California. Not here. Earthquakes and tsunamis. Radiation. Once the official had stapled her student visa into her passport and nodded her into Japan, she felt the fear. All her friends in school. Parties at the lake house, ski season in Europe, and Christmas in London.

At the carousel she looked again for the storyteller, but she couldn't see him in the line of bag watchers. When the luggage shuttled down the ramp she reached for her case and a strong hand came past her shoulder. For a moment she thought it was him, before a smiling American man said, "I got it."

She thanked him, righted the case and flicked out the handle, before wheeling it across the tiled floor like a faithful hound.

White gloved, and as expressionless as the man who'd stamped her passport, the customs official thumbed through the pages of her blue book, checked she'd ticked the box that said she wasn't transporting drugs or exotic reptiles, and welcomed her to Japan.

WE'RE ALL TIN-GOD psychologists, qualified or not, because anyone who announces they have the credentials to explain the vagaries of the human condition is an arrogant fool. And though I may have documented the social hierarchy of macaques on Ethiopian mountainsides, tagged Mumbai street dogs and followed their comings and goings via orbiting satellites and, as my colleagues often note, constructed theories on conformity that Hitler would have expounded, I'm an average father at best.

For all my papers and experiments, the lecture halls hushed by the weight of words, the false reverence for a man who amongst a host of talented peers was the one lucky enough to have a hit book, *Gangs, Groups and Belonging*, I'm baffled by the world my daughter will inherit. We're the mothers and fathers of an alien creed.

I could barely get Mazzy to look me in the eye the last time we'd met. My ex-wife's poison, I fooled myself. Not the fact I was dragging her from college in San Diego to a Tokyo International School.

"Have you seen that film about them killing dolphins?" she'd screamed down the phone when I told her a semester in Japan would be infinitely more educational than slouching around LA malls or Kensington High Street.

"Find out for yourself," I challenged. "It's everything you think it's not."

I read little about Japan before I first flew out here, nearly twenty years ago. Pages from my guidebook about population and climate, why not to leave chopsticks protruding from a bowl of rice. My brother had dropped me off at Heathrow on a wet and windy November morning. We shook hands and hugged at the check-in desk, then I watched him duck back into the rain and scuttle across the car park.

Although I wasn't leaving England for any particular reason, I wasn't staying for one either. Aged twenty-two, a psychology degree that was worthless without a masters, I needed money, experience.

I qualified as an English teacher and applied for the best paid job I could find, regardless of continent, and flew out to Fukuoka, a city on the southern island of a bubble-deflated Japan. A country I knew nothing about beyond the lazy stereotypes.

The flight was filled with sleeping Japanese students, kids plugged into Walkmans and folding into their seats. I did wonder what kind of mistake I'd made, until the plane banked over Fukuoka and the city blazed like gold bullion.

I arrived at my apartment in the dark, slept on a tatami mat and woke up with a mountain in my window. On my first foray beyond the front door I got lost and flagged down a passing salaryman.

"Train station?"

Spectacled and suited, the familiar caricature of an entire nation, he didn't speak a word of English. But he got the gist and beckoned me to follow, street after street, the opposite direction to where he'd been heading, ensuring I was safely delivered to the ticket gate. I bowed deeply as I said thank you, I knew to do that much. He was bowing too, as if he'd just presented me with a pair of Japan's finest rose-tinted glasses to view my new life.

By arriving in ignorance, no thought of what to expect, the culture shock was joy. Fresh fish and immaculate trains, bright blue winter skies, self-filling baths with chirpy voices announcing they were the perfect temperature. I read Mishima novels and Basho haiku. Sitting cross-legged and watching Seven Samurai without subtitles was akin to a religious conversion. Above all the welcome change and surprise was the calmness to public life, the absolute lack of menace which haunts an English street. Perceived or real. On losing my wallet I was that sure it would be returned I didn't cancel my credit card. Two days later it came through the door with a letter from the finder apologising for not being able to bring it round sooner.

Not that I'd discovered utopia. Commuting from a box apartment to a sodium-lit English school and reading the same text to the same students quickly became a clockwork routine. But the escapades where I had walk-on roles in modern fairy tales upended any tedium.

After a night drinking and singing with colleagues, dancing around a karaoke box with teachers from across the globe, men and women washed up in Japan for a multitude of reasons including debt, divorce, martial arts training, an obsession with Asian women or a religious desire to proliferate English syntax, I missed the last train.

No mobile phone. No address of a new found friend. I could either sleep in a park or walk 20km. I started hiking, planning to make my apartment by dawn for a shower and change of clothes before another day teaching. The highway cut through flooded rice paddies, and I trudged the narrow path between burning headlights and plains of water. Then it started to rain. Hard, fat, stinging drops. I was about to walk home in sodden clothes when, from the dazzle of a car beam, a woman appeared wearing a white T-shirt with a kitten print on the front.

She wasn't shocked to see me, the soon-to-be soaked *gaijin* by the side of a highway. She simply stopped in the middle of the path and thrust her umbrella into my palm. I insisted I was okay, but she insisted I wasn't, and grabbed my wrist and forced the handle into my grip. Once I had the umbrella she walked back, and I tell you this despite the risk of cliché, into the dark from which she had appeared.

Enchanted by this fable-like episode, I booked my first vacation.

Blooming first at the southernmost tip of Kyushu, the bright pink cherry blossom sweeps across Japan announcing the arrival of spring. A carnival atmosphere fills the parks and squares with parties and picnics, and I planned to make the most of this fleeting celebration by following the procession across the country.

I hitched to the hot-spring town of Beppu, before catching a ferry to the castle city of Matsuyama and heading off to explore the depths of rural Shikoku. The smallest and least populous of the four main islands, the rugged interior has avoided the urban sprawl of modern Japan. Famous for its noodles and the yearly visit of 100,000 pilgrims visiting 88 Buddhist temples in a set order, I felt like I was walking into the bygone landscape of a painted screen.

After a lift from the relative bustle of Matsuyama I was soon hiking along a clear and fast flowing river, winding its way between mountains covered in bright green firs. A fine rain began to fall and the peaks disappeared. Despite getting wet, it was perfect. I was walking through an ancient gorge, watching banks of mist drift down from the clouds and over the trees.

But reality struck my Zen moment. My plan of reaching the southern city of Kochi by nightfall would be impossible unless I picked up a ride. The sky had turned charcoal grey, and the side of the road was looking more and more inviting.

Then possibly the oldest man in Japan pulled up and beckoned me into his truck. Shrunken and grizzled without a tooth in his mouth, I found out he was a woodcutter when we drove up to his house and saw logs, hundreds of them, stacked up to the sagging eaves. He gestured crazy axe-chopping motions and patted his puffed out chest with pride.

Thankfully, he turned back to the main road and asked if my legs were strong.

"Strong?"

We rounded a blind corner and stopped by a Road Closed sign that guarded a brand new tunnel cut through the mountain. Although lit by strips of neon, it would be dark by the time I'd walked the ten kilometres to the exit. And no cars following to pick me up. The woodcutter waited and watched my face, his rheumy eyes fixed on mine. Then he climbed out of the truck and opened the tailgate. From a plastic bag he gave me two rice balls wrapped in cling film.

The decision to hike had been made.

I climbed over the barrier and turned to wave goodbye, but the woodcutter had already gone.

Inside the entrance rows of silver chairs faced a stage covered in red cloth for an opening ceremony. I stood at the microphone and tried the switch. No sound except the bunting rippling in the breeze. The tunnel was a triumph of Japanese engineering, every section flawless. If I'd spun around with my eyes closed I could have walked out the way I'd entered.

I sang as I walked, Neil Young and Bob Dylan, sending the lyrics along the length of the tunnel, as though each line were a train, and each word a carriage, before they dissipated into the sky beyond the exit.

It was dark when I emerged a few hours later. Silhouettes of pine trees, graphite peaks. The next tunnel I walked through wasn't illuminated, and I ventured into a black hole. Water dripped and splashed, my footsteps echoed. I groped along with my hands held out like a blind man.

After a few hundred metres I was sucked into a vacuum of sight and sound. No dripping water. My footsteps oddly silenced. I recalled caving in Wales, sitting in the depth of a mountain and switching out the lamp. Body vanishing with the bulb. There, my fellow cavers were a torch click away. Here, in the lonely dark, I could've transformed into a wisp of soul.

I wanted to turn around and hike back to the illuminated tunnel. I could sleep with the comfort of electricity, the buzzing neon. Just as I'd made the decision to return I noticed a tiny glow ahead. No colour except this hovering, ethereal whiteness.

I'd long stopped believing in spirits, but not in the ability of the mind to create one. I walked towards the dot of light, watching it grow, unsure if it was getting bigger because I was walking towards it, or because it was floating towards me.

It wasn't a ghost. Manufactured or real.

It was a vending machine oasis in the middle of nowhere. Across Japan humming refrigeration units wait ready to eject cold cans of glucose. And here was a loyal refreshment droid on the edge of an abandoned car park. I popped in the necessary coins, clunked out the tins and downed two energy drinks. I walked on air for an hour before my batteries died.

As I was looking for a bush to shelter under the only car I'd seen since the woodcutter pulled over.

A kimono salesman took me all the way to Kochi, thrilled at the chance to practice his broken English while his precious dresses swayed on hangers above the back seat. Although I'd received only generosity and kindness travelling Japan, nothing had prepared me for the moment he untied a drawstring bag and emptied dozens of pearls onto his palm, rolled them around then picked out two. Placing them carefully into my cupped hands he'd said, *"Omiyage."* Souvenir. From our two languages I worked out he was telling me to give them to my bride on my wedding day.

I'm not superstitious, but perhaps if I hadn't lost them, somewhere between the Japanese countryside and the Nevada desert, I'd still be married.

三

KOJI OKADA CLOSED his eyes and waited for her to sleep. In his dark reverie she seemed phosphorescent, almost burning. He waited for the cabin lights to dim and then he opened his eyes. She was curled in her seat. Bare feet pulled up from the floor. He studied her red-painted toenails. Blood jewels in the screen light. He wanted to draw the blanket over their nakedness.

Abruptly, he stood and opened the luggage rack. He checked the aisles, the dead rows of dreaming passengers.

Then he ripped the tag off her bag, snapping the plastic cord. He took down his briefcase and walked to the rear of the plane and sat in a spare window seat. Once more he looked to the shock-mouthed O of the dazzling moon, the two of them face to face, before he shut the blind and went to the lavatory.

He slid back the latch, put down the seat and studied her handwriting. Her name.

四

WE ROSE ABOVE Tokyo in a flying car. On the apex of Rainbow Bridge, a span of steel and concrete tall enough for container ships and oil tankers to cruise beneath, I watched the cityscape loom.

"Japanese engineering," stated my driver, Professor Yamada, noting my focus on the rivets and cables stretching towards the sun.

"I had a Toyota Corolla," I told him. "When I was a student. Every time it rained I had to jump start it."

Yamada shook his head.

"I always parked facing downhill if the weather looked bad."

"No, no," said Yamada. "Japanese car. Built by British worker."

He laughed, that sonorous bass. With his long black hair and white teeth he looked like a cartoon villain. Not that I'd have shared this thought with him, eminent social psychologist at Tokyo University, colleague and mentor, driving me to collect Mazzy from the station.

"She wanted to ride the train herself," I said, checking my watch, again, and wondering if I'd done the right thing by letting her ride the airport shuttle rather than wait at the terminal. "She told me she wasn't a child any more."

Yamada apologised, before explaining that the welcome ceremony for international staff couldn't be rearranged.

"The Japanese responsibility to company before family."

Once more we went through the formalities of his apology and my dismissal of its necessity.

"Anyway," I said. "This is the deal on her coming to Japan. That I'm not going to babysit her twenty four hours a day."

"Is she," Yamada paused, searched the neural database of his phrases. "The apple of your eye?"

"She is. But her mother has made her a little sour."

Generally, Yamada's English was excellent, and I was wary of correcting him unless his idiom was so arcane that Dickens would have thought it outdated. Or his earnest phrasing was a comical faux pas. At a reception in London he'd daintily lifted a china cup from its saucer and announced to our hostess that it was an 'adequate' tea.

"When I last visited the UK, I was very shocked."

Yamada changed the subject, avoided talk of family and divorce, the private life bared.

"You have forsaken community for authority of law. Security cameras. Speed cameras. Garbage police. The riots were no surprise."

I wasn't about to begin defending the ills of British society. I could hardly argue with him. Once the smoke had settled on the charred city centres, a broadsheet editor asked me to contribute a piece on mob psychology. In the article I'd argued that the increasing number of cults, sects and churches, along with a splintering of political values in parties across the globe, as well as the bands of British kids in delinquent union, were symptomatic of rifts in society, a lack of belonging.

The familiar, terrifying sway of the crowd. A phenomenon I've been obsessed with since watching the Asch inspired drumbeat experiment, where a group of subjects were simply asked to count the number of times a drum was struck. Six people listened to a drum beaten eight times. Five of the six subjects were confederates planted by the researchers, and when asked how many times the drum had been struck, each replied, "Seven." The guinea pig, in almost all of the tests, conformed with the group despite believing he or she had actually, and correctly, counted eight.

When the terror cell pledges deathly allegiance, it is with flesh and blood they are bound. Not the seemingly tangible god.

Although gangs of youths burning and stealing was hardly original, the summer riots forced a change in my angle on group theory. We needed the positives of crowd psyche. When a third opportunity to return to Japan appeared in my in-box, a focus on the power of community and co-operation, rather than the twisted eccentricities of the cult lives I'd previously studied, I phoned Mazzy and began the negotiations to convince her, and her mother, that a radioactive country recovering from an earthquake and a tidal wave was going to be home for the next six months.

**

Since the divorce ten years ago, a wrangling that only US courts could have choreographed, Mazzy had lived with her mother just outside of San Diego.

We did love each other, once. Lydia and I. Fiercely, with an intellectual passion as much as any physical desire. When she proposed the clause of sharing royalties on any books or papers I'd written while we were married, I simply accepted, much to the attorney's chagrin, as her influence on my thinking was undeniable.

Though it certainly wasn't love at first sight.

We met on the driveway of a house in Santa Fe. Beyond a sprinkled lawn and a white door framed by fake Roman columns, in a carefully constructed dormitory of aluminium bunk beds and flat-pack closets, lay 39 men and women dressed in black trousers and black shirts, brand new Nike trainers. Over each of their faces lay a square of purple cloth. Mostly they were young, healthy and intelligent. IT professionals and budding lawyers, graduates from Ivy League schools.

And members of Heaven's Gate.

All but two had eaten an apple sauce cyanide and washed it down with vodka, dying in organised shifts so each following group could wrap plastic bags over their heads to ensure suffocation, and prepare their souls to be gathered by an interstellar ship tailing the Hale-Bopp comet.

My first post after the PhD was assisting a research project in Los Angeles, devising exit strategies for gang members, and I knew Lydia from a lecture I'd attended at Berkeley. An admired cult specialist, she was the go-to expert for news desks reporting on criminal clans. Now she'd been called in to help document a death scene. When I stepped past a cop and dropped the name of her department colleague, she turned and asked, "And you are?"

Then she was waved through the police tape while I stood with the gawkers on the pavement.

I'd driven up on a tip off from one of her students, the news piquing my morbid fascination with mass suicide. I was a student of Waco and Jonestown, had devoured accounts from surviving members, pored over the details of cult life and read the warped manifestos, and then, finally, the police reports of the flaming and tragic showdowns.

However, my immature curiosity turned to shock and anger when paramedics wheeled out the bodies.

Lydia had been allowed inside the house, the morgue. The next day I sent her an email apologising for my crass introduction. She didn't reply for a month, and then asked if I could meet her that afternoon at a highway diner near San Diego.

I took a booth seat by the window. Got there early and watched a bad coffee cool on the Formica table. Before she walked across the car park and into the diner. The force of her in a room. That long, glossy hair, pinned back by her sunglasses. A dark, wild lustre, inherited from a native American grandmother in British Columbia.

We said our hellos and sat down, both apologising for being rude at our first meeting.

"I was playing up my credentials to the police," she explained. "I knew what a coup it was to get in there." She shook her head. "But I wasn't expecting that. The neatness. How ordered the killing was."

She wanted to talk to another professional about the disciple's final subversion. How a group gains the consciousness of the individual. She tried to be clinical in her explanation, the hypotheses and arguments. Names of researchers. I nodded. Professor Lifton's characteristics of mind control: the demand for purity, doctrine over person, sacred science and the dispensing of existence. She waved away the standards with exasperated gestures, and I offered what empathy I could when her voice wobbled. She was older, more qualified, but had stood in a room full of bodies.

"Come on." she said. "You talk. Tell me something."

That flowing, raven hair, still damp from a swim.

"Why were you driving up to death scenes on a sunny afternoon?"

I told her about visiting the Masada fort in Israel when I was a schoolboy, reading dusty plaques about the hundreds who killed themselves, and their children, rather than surrender to the Romans.

"They saw a comet to jump on." She shook her head. "Bad joke. What else got you into watching sheep."

"My fear of crowds."

"That's a new one."

I confessed I was both terrified and intrigued by a group soul. Whatever the intentions. That I hated demonstrations, and could only play team sports if I was captain.

"That's like saying you'll only be the citizen of a country if you can be President."

"Dictator."

She laughed. Bluntly she asked if I was married, and when I said no she made a joke that single life is a dictatorship where one person is happy, and that married life is a democracy where compromise means nobody is.

"I could compromise."

She smiled. A spark to her brown eyes, a playful twinkle. It was the hint of a flirt, a study of my face.

Later, she'd tell me she was guessing my age. She was wrong. She thought I was older. But it didn't matter then. Or the next weekend. The age gap was a thrill for us both, sitting on the porch of her house outside San Diego, the faint, orange glow of a bushfire in the silver mountains. A bottle of wine in the ice box. We could hear coyotes howling in the dark, the hum of an occasional car winding through the darkened valley.

I was, I still am, a young father. I was twenty six and she was thirty four. Hardly on the last ticking of her biological clock, she made it clear she was too old to be fooling around with men cutting notches into bedposts.

"Handle it," she'd challenged, on a drive to the Grand Canyon three months into our relationship. "I want a family, and you need to know that before we get into something that eats up years."

I was going through a euphoric period when she threw down the gauntlet. I cycled to work and sat in an office that overlooked a tree lined campus. Lunched on a rooftop that offered views of the sapphire Pacific. Mid afternoons I drank coffee with a woman who was beautiful, thrilling, and whip smart. She'd conjure up theories and destroy revered ideas in the same breath.

"We have something here, Ben, you know that. But I'm not fooling around, getting old and bitter because I didn't have kids."

She was driving. Sunglasses on. All that sky and desert reflected in the lenses.

"Well?"

The window was down, her hair whipped around her face.

"You're driving too fast for me to jump out."

It was a stupid remark.

"Okay," she said, checking the rear view mirror. "Go on. Do it." She slowed down to thirty, tires thudding over the rumble strips.

"I'll raise you a wedding."

The car juddered along the edge of the highway.

"Look out."

She swerved from a prang with signpost before accelerating back onto the asphalt, revving the engine hard.

"You're bluffing."

"We could drive into Vegas tonight, and wake up tomorrow man and wife."

Lydia drove on, chewed her bottom lip. "Neither of us do God, so what does a piece of paper mean to anyone but the IRS?"

"Last of the romantics."

"Ben, stop fucking with me. Especially while I'm driving."

We drove into Las Vegas after sundown, the whole neon shebang calling us from the desert like some gaudy mirage that didn't vanish when we arrived. Beneath the flashing bulbs and coloured fountains, we sat in backed up traffic with kitsch limousines and tour buses, hotel shuttles filled with Chinese gamblers. I wound down the window and listened to a gaggle of Geordie women argue about the price of a helicopter tour.

We checked into a hotel, walked rows of clunking slot machines and watched four consecutive sunsets blaze and fade on the roof of a miniature Venice. Then, after sharing a bottle of champagne, we walked into the 9th Street Elvis Chapel and bought the Hound Dog wedding package.

五

AFTER THE PLANE taxied to a halt, and the cabin doors hissed open to Japan, Koji stood quickly and scanned the aisle.

There she was.

Luminous above the dark heads.

He lost sight of her while he waited to exit. Passengers with bags and belongings. Fools with duty free and branded shopping. He pushed past a tall American man who told him to wait his turn. He thought about the man fighting for breath, drowning in his grip.

Koji needn't have rushed, panicked. She was delayed at passport control. The line of foreigners entering the country was longer than the line of returning Japanese, and he was waved through before her without a question asked.

Lingering in the corridor to the baggage hall, he stared at the planes through the window. Jet liners nosing into the terminals. Like toys. He'd wanted to be a pilot, once. When she passed by he watched her reflection on the glass.

Then the empty, revolving carousels. Koji stood beside a pillar while the passengers waited for their cases to appear. They switched on phones or yawned. She looked around the hall, at signs and at people. He liked the way she flicked her hair over one side of her head.

He pulled her tag from his pocket. Again, he studied her name, tracing the looped writing with his fingertip.

When he next looked up the luggage had appeared. The tall American man lifted her suitcase onto the tiled floor. He smiled. She smiled too. Bright, white teeth. A pink doll mouth.

Then she wheeled her suitcase towards customs, beaming at the official. He briefly checked her passport, and then gave it back. She bowed, a little awkwardly, and walked into Japan.

He followed, waiting on the marked line as the gloved official checked his declaration form. Koji watched him read. He was young. Perhaps they were the same age. The official checked his passport. Compared photo and flesh. He asked Koji about Los Angeles, whether he'd bought any souvenirs for his family. Koji watched his Adam's apple move as he talked. It was too large for his thin neck, and he wanted to slit his throat and see what came out.

Koji answered the question. He told the official his mother and father were dead.

The official closed his passport and returned it held in both hands. Then he waved him through to arrivals.

Koji didn't expect to see her alone. Walking away from the express train counter, the ticket in her hand like a fan.

六

WAITING AT THE gates in Tokyo station. An ice-cold melt in my sternum. The fear, when I realised Mazzy's phone wouldn't connect, and that if she didn't get on the right train I'd be flapping around searching for her on the biggest transport system in the world. Bumped and nudged in the criss-crossing tangents of zipping commuters, I cursed out loud. At myself. Too eager to please, swayed by the will of my teenage daughter.

I checked my watch against the clock on the concourse, the confirmation she was late. I imagined phoning Lydia, the accusations and apologies.

Then she was there at the barrier.

"Dad."

Waving and smiling. Remembering she was supposed to be mad at me for press-ganging her to Japan.

In the reluctant hug, was love. I could feel it in the give of her shoulders, see it in her sparky blue eyes, ours, not her mother's. Yet how strange and disconcerting to see her older when I leaned back and looked her up and down. Only six months, but the girl had gone and the woman was beckoning.

"I'm not going to make you eat dolphin."

She shrugged. "I'm over that. It's the radiation I'm supposed to watch out for."

More college kid than high school. The backpack exchanged for a wheeled suitcase and designer handbag.

"I didn't know you could see plutonium with the naked eye."

"Mom's gonna mail with a list of foods to avoid."

I didn't hear myself tut.

"Don't tut so loud."

But Mazzy did.

We jumped in a taxi, talked about the flight and school. I hated these first conversations, stilted like old colleagues or distant relatives. The awkward settling in before the father-daughter dynamic returned. Knowing that the more we spoke the quicker the paternal atmosphere would resume, I improvised my knowledge on Tokyo, a bogus tour guide.

"I've got all sorts of cool places to show you," I gushed, sounding like a boy trying to impress on a date rather than the father regaining his daughter. "Did you study any Japanese?"

After a jet-lag nap on the sofa, I showed Mazzy the sights and sounds of Shibuya. Brash and neon. The ebb and flow of the famous crossing, the never-ending crowds teeming from the station as if the millipede steps of a single being. We walked past the hair-sprayed pimps beckoning women to hostess at clubs. We lingered beneath the tower-sized screens illuminating drunken salarymen, the gangs of schoolgirls hitching skirts, shoppers parading designer labels, and a cane-tapping blind man parting the flood. All of them intermittently photographed by a dumbstruck tourist with his lens to the lights.

Then we sat and observed from a café window. The hypnotic waves of bobbing heads. Young and old in a capital that shuttles rather than jostles. Mazzy seemed quiet, but I hoped she was excited by the city she was about to make home.

She did perk up for a while, asked questions about bowing, how to say thank you. Whether she could get California roll in Tokyo.

Or it could've just been the caffeine from her double-shot that upped her interest in the country she'd fought to avoid living in. Because an hour later, on the 30th floor of the Metropolitan Building, an H-shaped tower with views from Yokohama Bay to the white tipped peak of Mount Fuji, she cried.

"Hey, hey." I put my arm on her shoulder.

"I'm not supposed to be here."

A flock of Korean tourists swiftly moved through the viewing area, pulling down souvenirs and spinning back through the turnstiles.

"Don't be silly."

"I don't know anyone."

"Come on," I said. "I'll treat you to some of the best sushi in Tokyo."

But her head and stomach were still in LA. We rode the lift down to the business district, and before I could hail a cab she saw a Sizzler and marched us inside, slouching on a leather booth seat and sulking over her iPhone between handfuls of nachos.

"I told you. It won't connect to a Japanese network."

"They have iPhones here, I've seen them."

"They call it Galapagos."

"What?"

"Their network evolved separately."

"This place is fucked."

I told her not to swear.

I told her she needed to step up and be an adult, that she was no longer a child.

"So I should be making my own decisions."

I sighed, deflated. "Give a little. Please."

Neither of us could sleep that night. I lay in bed listening to her pad around the apartment, imagining I was her, looking out of the window onto the city. What did I see? What did I want from it all? What did I think of my father?

She'd relaxed a little after the Sizzler restaurant, when I'd taken her into a Japanese phone shop and connected her to the pixel world of her peers, the light-fired comment and gossip that's rewiring our youth's neurones beyond anything my analogue generation can imagine and, increasingly, compete with. We frustrate our children asking how to find an address or download music, which button takes the photo. Still, she knew the rules around her father, and that if the phone came out at the dinner table or in a conversation it would be confiscated. And though she did follow protocol, I knew that with each mail, tweet, like, poke and ping, the social norms of my generation were being eradicated. What fool would bet on recognising the world at the end of the century.

I was dozing when I heard a voice. Not hers.

I woke from a half-dream where Tokyo had stopped. Paused. Each and every commuter, shopper, salaryman and high school student freeze-framed.

Then again that voice.

Mazzy was talking to Lydia on Skype. My bedroom door was shut, but both my window and Mazzy's were open, and there was no mistaking her mother.

"Mazzy," she said. "We discussed this."

"You did with dad, but not me. And whose fucking life is it."

"Mazzy."

I got up and put on my dressing gown. Then I pushed open Mazzy's door without knocking.

"What the fuck, dad."

She was sat cross-legged on the bed, her iPad on the dresser. And Lydia, right there. Her whole face on the screen, in the room.

"Ben?"

"Who else?"

"Sit down. All I can see is your crotch."

I sat, and asked Lydia if she let Mazzy swear in the house.

"Don't start."

"If you two argue this computer's going out the window."

"We promise, Ben, don't we."

"We do."

"Happy families," said Mazzy.

"Don't be glib," warned Lydia.

For the first time in years, possibly ever, we sat around and talked things out together. Almost. Lydia, from what looked like her study in California, joined forces with me to convince our daughter that six months in Japan would be good for her.

"You mean good for you two."

Ex-husband and ex-wife, united. We needed each other in battle. Mazzy cried and swore, threatened that she'd get on a plane to London, and that if we forced her to go to school here she'd, "Sit in class like a fucking zombie."

The turning point was a speech from Lydia, on how proud she already was of her daughter, and that after her own parents had sent her to Canada for a summer while they sailed around the Caribbean she came back a smarter, more independent woman. No longer a girl.

Finally, Mazzy agreed to be in Tokyo for at least a month. "A trial," she stated. "Then I get to decide my own future."

Lydia said, "Thank you, Ben." And I thought her as condescending as ever. Eight years older than me but eternally wiser. I asked Mazzy to put the kettle on while I talked to her mother.

"A conference call about me, without me."

"You make better coffee."

She looked at the screen for permission. "Skype me tomorrow."

"Love you."

Lydia wore a black track top, her hair tied up in a ponytail.

I said, "We got that sorted."

"For the moment."

"Thanks. For your support."

She shrugged. "Ultimately, it's her decision. But I swear if one of those reactors starts leaking then she's on the first plane back."

I nodded to the camera, to the mother of our child.

"And that's my decision."

"*Hai. Wakarimashita.*" I bowed.

"Don't be childish."

"That's Japanese for yes, and that I understand."

Lydia glared at the camera. Through the screen, across a continent, and into my eyes. "Look after her, Ben."

**

Her long black hair would fall over her toned shoulders when she walked from the surf with her brown skin gleaming. A champion swimmer at college, trips to the beach were spent building sandcastles with Mazzy while her mother cut waves and dived like an oiled and sleek cormorant. I'd look to the glitter and static of the bright surface, see her shadow vanish, and turn back to the grand plans of a two year old builder and her foot deep moat.

Mazzy would hold up dull, chipped treasure. "Look daddy." And a broken shell from an ancient sea would be the most prized object in the world.

Washing the salt from Mazzy's hair, wrapping her in a towel and watching the sunset blaze over the porch while she gurgled and tried her first words.

There were times I sat in her room while she was sleeping, studying the rise and fall of her tiny chest, a feathery sigh, the cow lick curls across her forehead. Part of me wished to leap into the future and see a confident young woman striding across a campus. I wanted to jump from the permanent anxiety of fatherhood into the knowledge of a job well done.

And this was before the wave.

It was a bright, windy day. Lydia went for a swim, but the tussling currents had been too much for even her muscular strokes, and she'd come in breathless after only ten minutes.

"That's one feisty ocean," she said, grabbing the drink bottle.

"We'll just paddle," I said. "Ankle deep."

"Toe deep," she warned.

We were, I swear to this very day, paddling in the foam, not even in the wash of breaking waves.

I had my back turned to the sea.

"What the fuck were you looking at?" I'd later be asked.

"A dog," I told Lydia.

"A fucking dog."

I was watching a dog leap and catch a frisbee, as was Mazzy, when I was slammed so hard from behind that I thought someone had run up and tackled me. I had Mazzy's hand, but would've pulled her arm off if I hadn't let go.

I remember sand in my mouth, clutching, reaching, grabbing. Water, not Mazzy. Her tiny body in the brunt of tide. When the wave slid back to the sea I found my feet. Mazzy was tumbling like a bundle of laundry in a washing machine, sucked into the white teeth of the next breaking wave.

I ran, waded.

Lydia hurdled past me, high-stepping the swirl before diving into the mouth that swallowed her daughter. After the rush of shattered wave, she appeared, rose from the surf with Mazzy in her arms. A whole ocean defeated. She fought off another wave which tried, and failed again, to snatch what it had very nearly claimed.

Mazzy coughed and spluttered. Where there'd been no lifeguards there were now bronzed men sprinting. "She's bleeding," someone said. Possibly me. People were told to stand back. A jeep pulled up and Lydia got in the passenger seat with Mazzy in her arms. I held onto the side rail with another lifeguard. I couldn't even tell you if it was a man or woman.

What I do know is that Lydia carried Mazzy from the medical centre, the cut on her ear sealed with a Band-Aid. She kissed her head again and again. "Mazzy, baby."

I drove home while Lydia cried. When we got back to the house Mazzy was asleep and Lydia carried her into the front room and laid her on the sofa and told me to get a blanket.

**

"You got me chocolate for mochas?"

I walked away from the screen, Lydia, and into the kitchen where Mazzy was opening cupboards.

"I did."

"Thanks, dad."

In the east above the towers, a vein of gold cracked the overcast sky. I slid open the doors and stepped onto the balcony, watching crows swoop between the rooftops. Mazzy brewed the coffee and carried the mugs outside.

"What did mom say?"

"That she loved me."

"You're being sarcastic."

"So she doesn't?"

"Dad." She passed over the mocha. "Strong and sweet."

I took the mug and sipped. "We won't be going back to sleep after these."

Buzzed on caffeine and resolutions, I called a taxi and took Mazzy to the Tsukiji fish market. We watched the trawlers dock with loaded nets, how the salt depth dripped from gleaming scales and pooled on the cobbles like low tide. Lobsters and crabs escaped from polystyrene boxes, crawling between the steps of fishmongers and buyers, chefs from restaurants haggling over cuts of tuna and catches of salmon. A truck drove away filled with squid. Through the windows we saw the transparent bodies of negligee pink, an alien fleet sailing into a sushi knife ambush. Mazzy was rapt. She stopped and studied tanks of sea urchins. Mesmerised by an old woman with eels in her fists like currents of dark.

When we sat and had breakfast at a nearby family restaurant she took out her sketchpad and started drawing. Goggle-eyed fish and lobster claws. The rubber-suited men with flashing knives.

She could always draw, but her talent had matured. I picked up a Daily Yomiuri and pretended to read while she shaded scales and fins. I wanted her to know how amazed I was by her rendering, how proud, but needed to get the compliment right so I didn't sound like the condescending parent praising the average. She'd spot a fake comment, always had. "That scepticism is your English DNA," Lydia had once told me. "Not mine."

Mazzy turned the pad and showed me a squid, hovered in the dark window of the aquarium truck, eyes flecked with light.

"You should draw everyday," I said. "I'll throw away my camera if you capture the world like this."

She spun the pad, considered her creation. "I'll come back with my colours."

In the taxi home I told her the folk story of Urashima Taro, the fisherman who saves a turtle being teased by a group of boys. When another turtle comes ashore the next day, and tells him the turtle he rescued was the daughter of the Sea Emperor, he's granted gills to swim down to the underwater palace of the Dragon God. Here he meets the turtle he saved, a princess, of course. After a few days together Urashima Taro tells the princess he has to go back to the surface world, and she gives him a magical box that will protect him, but which he must never open. Back in his town he finds that all the people he knew have vanished. He recognises no one, and when he asks after his own name he's told the ancient story of a fisherman who drowned at sea. In his three days underwater, three hundred years have passed on land. Overwhelmed by grief, he opens the magical box and is engulfed by a cloud of smoke, turning his beard white and crooking his back. A voice from the sea, the princess, tells him that the box contained his old age.

Mazzy listened, nodded and waited. "And?"

"And what?"

"That's it?"

"The end. In some versions he turns to dust because no one can live three hundred years."

"Where's the happily ever after?"

"Not in a Japanese fairy tale."

"Have you heard the one about the moon princess?"

"*Kaguya-hime*?"

"It's beautiful."

"Where did you hear that?"

"Some guy on the plane."

"Some guy?"

"A Japanese guy. We were looking at the moon above the clouds, and he told me about *Kaguya-hime*."

"How old was he? This guy."

Mazzy shook her head, incredulous. "*Dad*," she pleaded.

I left it there, abruptly. We'd had a good morning, and could do without a missile of fatherly paranoia.

七

KOJI HAD SAT in the same carriage as Mazzy on the express train into Tokyo. Four rows back. He studied how she watched the flashing countryside, the bamboo thickets and anonymous suburbs. How a city assembled on tinted glass. He followed her all the way to the ticket barrier at Tokyo station where her father, of this he was sure, hugged his daughter.

Koji had patience.

He once sat in the White Room of the group house for a week. Longer than any of the others.

A white room. White walls, floors and ceiling. White screws in the light fittings. He wore a linen gown and white gloves. He was forbidden to look at his own skin. They brought him one bowl of rice a day. Dressed in white. Veiled. He ate from a white bowl with ivory chopsticks, and the only colour he saw was his urine and excrement.

On the seventh day two of the younger women came into the room and knelt before him. One of them carried a large glass vial. She held it while the other drew apart his gown. She took hold of his penis and masturbated him into the container. They carried his semen from the room and closed the door.

Later, Koji could not tell if it was night or day, The Leader slid back the screen and told him to stand. She was old, feeble. Dying from electromagnetic waves. Yet she knew which day the world would end, and that extra-terrestrials would ferry them to refuge. She beckoned Koji to follow her along the sodium lit corridor. He smelled dying flesh beneath her thin gown, and his own seed on her papery skin.

He'd once been chosen.

Wanted.

八

TWO WEEKS AFTER the divorce was settled in a San Diego courthouse, I left LA and landed in the drizzle of Heathrow.

Five years in California. An ex-wife and a beautiful daughter. After the wave our family had lasted six months. Even though it was finished the moment Lydia had come arrowing past me into the sea.

Boxes of books arrived at my parents, the divided CD collection. A country and a marriage were no more than images fired along my synapses. Apart from the single page letters, the felt-tip pictures mailed weekly by my little Mazzy.

I moved into a scruffy flat on the unfashionable side of Notting Hill, and spent my new life stuttering along the Central Line between Shepherd's Bush and Holborn. From a canyon filled with sage and buckwheat, the Pacific rollers steady on the golden shore, my daughter in my arms, to a damp room on the edge of a council estate.

With a research team funded by the Football Association and MET police, I was collating data on crowd control techniques. I studied films of wayward hooligans then commuted home to walk past gangs of spitting youths stalking west London. Videos of mobs torching cars and smashing windows, the burliest thugs yanking designer dresses off worried mannequins – the grainy archives, before an updated summer of fire and riots was digitised and recorded on phones and cameras.

This was stock footage from the 70s, men in flares throwing bricks and bottles. "The good old days," remarked a former organiser we'd paid to explain game day tactics and the syncopation of mob violence, outwitting the police to get the fight they'd spent all week planning.

He smoked a pack of Superkings and harked back as if he were the victorious revolutionary ousting a stubborn dictatorship, while I took pages of notes on essentially the same scene: the to and fro rush of police versus crowd, before an eventual numbers dominance, or a cavalry charge of mounted officers, cleared the street.

The Football Association had paid us to find solutions, to qualify the use of maximum force with the least manpower, and my flash of inspiration came from a need to end the project early as much as any eureka moment. First I contacted the American Beef council, who in turn put me through to the Texas Ranchers Association. We paid for a cowboy to fly out to a sports hall in Reading and corral hordes of undergraduates running from one end to the other. He showed us that with minimum policing a rampaging crowd could be contained in the same way a stampeding herd of cattle could be brought to a halt.

I presented our findings to the MET and shook hands with my research assistants. We soon heard reports of effective crowd control, half a dozen officers penning fifty football fans threatening to riot. The basis of our strategy was a miniature divide and conquer, a technique that would evolve to control G8 demonstrations with water cannons. Kettling. Not a phrase we hatched, or a method we officially condoned.

The divorce, losing my daughter, and a move back to England for a grim winter in a windowless lab, had taken all the joy from life. When I observed people, groups, cults and cliques, the ugly dysfunctions of a failing community, I was a student with no empathy for my subject. As if all the human parts of the world could be stripped down and examined like a car in a Haynes manual.

I held out till January, and then flew to see Mazzy as arranged with Lydia. I had my little girl for three days. I picked her up from Del Mar and drove north towards Yosemite, one hand on the wheel, and one hand on Mazzy's soft hair as she slept.

I drove a horizon. Space. The car seemed to be getting smaller as the vista stretched into sky. I woke Mazzy because I thought we might shrink into nothing if I kept on driving without speaking.

"Want some juice?"

"No."

"Milkshake?"

She shook her head. She looked from her elevated child seat to the low, scrub hills. Already she thought like me, suffered from the same waking grouchiness. Aged three she had to rebuild the world and its purpose each time she woke from a nap. Her mother would be ready for the day and all its dramas the moment she awoke.

"We're going to see some really, really huge trees," I enthused.

She had an electronic piano that played the sounds of different farm animals. I heard mooing cows and oinking pigs in reply. Barely speaking, and she already knew how to shun.

I drove on, pointing out horses in fields, birds on house roofs, that kind of thing. Still, she prodded the toy and looked away.

Then I broke the stalemate, and my principles, with a stop at McDonalds. A Happy Meal truce. Plastic toys and florid food. The company of other kids in the junk food madhouse of a thousand plastic balls and a creaking slide.

She skipped across the parking lot, climbed into her seat, and danced a moulded clown along the dashboard. I pulled onto the highway, a tingling, tremulous joy. From a babble of random words, the muddle of imagined conversation that toddlers can entertain themselves with for hours, she burst into London's Burning. She sang the rhyme all the way through, before I joined in on the verse behind, and the two of us sang in a raucous round, over and over, louder and louder, until we were shouting and laughing together.

There would be photos in the snow at the lodge.

A glimpsed, lone coyote. Padding through drifts outside the window.

The two of us standing on a rock before the majestic granite of El Capitan.

But no bittersweet moment would haunt me more than singing in the car.

I drove Mazzy home and sat with Lydia in the kitchen. At a counter I'd fitted myself, carrying the ten foot length of pine from the truck with her uncle. She was already seeing someone else. A pair of men's hiking boots in the cupboard. I didn't dare raise the matter of who was touching my daughter, the thought alone made me sure I was capable of murder. There was nothing to say. Or there was too much to begin. I simply reported on what we'd done and where we'd been.

"I'm glad you had this time with her, Ben."

Lydia had lost weight, painted her nails.

"But that doesn't mean you get the summer."

I'd proposed that Mazzy stay with me in London during June, and that I'd join my brother and his kids at a cottage in Norfolk for most of July.

"It's not about you."

"I know it's not."

"You can't ship her across time zones."

"She sleeps when she wants, anyway."

"Great. She'll be awake all night and nap through kindergarten."

We sat and got nowhere. Or I got nowhere. Stability and bonding, home. The keywords in her defence. Or was she the prosecutor? I wondered if Lydia was afraid I'd snatch her away for good. That Mazzy would land in England and never see her mother again.

I said, "Do you think I'm going to kidnap her or something? Is that it?"

Lydia laughed. Dismissed the suggestion with a wave of her hand. "No, no. God, you fly over here for a weekend, play in the snow and feed her burgers, and then think you could manage the day to day care alone."

"Don't start."

"It's on your resume."

"What fucking resume?"

"Your glorious parenting."

Then began the fire, the flames of argument and blame. Back to the moment on the beach, the father who let go of his daughter.

Mazzy woke up, cried, and then ran upstairs to her room, slamming the door with all her tiny might.

九

WHEN KOJI STILL dreamed of cities, and the dreams were the glittering visions of a boy obsessed with manga and science fiction, he sat at the same wooden table in the same wooden house his father and grandfather had sat before. He ate rice, fish and miso soup. His grandmother poured more tea into his cup when it was empty. She shuffled across the tatami in her worn out slippers, talking to herself or reciting conversations from a different century. She woke at dawn every morning, creaking down the stairs into the dark kitchen. Her actions were automatic after fifty years of rising before her husband, even after he died, to cook his breakfast and boxed lunch.

Koji's mother cleaned office buildings and his father was a security guard on a construction site in Kobe. The three of them in a two room apartment. Weekends Koji rode the train back to his grandparents' scrapyard, playing in the twisted metal and broken cars. All around the house, beyond the rusting fence and pot-holed driveway, the fields teemed with rice. His grandmother wobbled the dusty paths, balancing jugs of iced tea for the hired labour, back bent over and swaddled against the sun. She watched them pick and plant, wagged her gnarled fingers and spun folk tales about devils in the hills.

She moved to Kobe from Tokyo after the great quake of 1923. She spoke about it as though it had happened yesterday. Confused by recent events, yet lucid in the past. She told Koji about a city of oil lamps and paper screen doors, the great wooden temples. "What the earth left standing, fire ravaged."

Koji's mother and father had been ash since January 17th 1995. Many knew the date. It was the morning of the Great Hanshin earthquake, when tremors rippled beneath the port city and shook buildings to dust.

Koji had woken in a room that wobbled like jelly. He called out for his mother and father, but neither were home. He ran outside in his pyjamas, between the rubble and bleeding people, the fallen signs and sparking cables. A toppled highway. How strange to see a vacant taxi slewed to a halt in the middle of a road, pedestrians crossing on a red signal. He thought he saw a policeman wearing a scarlet Kabuki mask, and then realised it was blood.

Rescue teams were already clambering on the debris in search of survivors. A salaryman, still wearing his shirt and tie, helped a fireman carry a woman to an ambulance. She could've been any secretary in any office, her company uniform powdered with dust. She was as loose as a doll when they laid her on the stretcher.

He never saw his parents' bodies. His mother was scrubbing toilets in a ten-storey block that snapped like a dead tree. His father wasn't guarding a construction site. He died watching pornography, inhaling smoke from a noodle shop that had caught fire above a basement cinema.

Koji moved in with his grandmother. She was all he had. He was all she had. When she remembered who he was. Afternoons he came home and found her talking to his dead father. Then she'd talk to Koji as if he were her son. A pantomime routine of fear. Koji running home from school, his grandmother waiting for him, his father. Angry if he was late. Dismissing his homework with a brush or a mop, the list of chores. The crone and the orphan. The couple who slept in the same futon until Koji was in his teens, curled like a cat at his grandmother's feet.

"YOU'VE GOT TWENTY minutes," I called to Mazzy through the bathroom door.

Yamada planned to welcome her to Japan with a *nabe* feast, and had invited us to his house in Omori, a down town neighbourhood near Shinagawa.

"And the Japanese punctuality stereotype is true."

"I heard you the first time."

Mazzy had already unpacked, hung clothes and scattered make up on the dresser. While she was in the shower I snooped around her room. T-shirts folded, jeans and a skirt on the back of her chair. Her sketchbook. When she was a child this was also my territory. Every nook and cranny of her space, my space. Now I felt like a soldier behind enemy lines, a secret agent with the threat of death if caught opening a drawer, turning the page of her journal.

When the shower stopped I slipped back into the living room. Guilty. Proud and scared. I'd missed a transformation somewhere between London and LA. A point where the girl I carried on my shoulders, the girl who cried if her teddy fell on the floor, was buying lipstick and lacy underwear.

She got dressed and I stood on the balcony and thought about Freud. It's all well and good to stand back and pontificate on the burgeoning sexuality of one's own progeny, but by god try watching other men leer at your daughter while walking her down the street.

We were on the train to Yamada's when I slipped in the question of boyfriends.

"I don't want to talk about it."

"I'm allowed to ask."

She shrugged, looked at the train map.

"Your mum said there was someone called Josh."

"Dad," she said through gritted teeth. "Forget it."

Passengers looked up from their books. Perhaps they'd understood every word. Or not a single one. Deciphered the body language, the matching eyes. The teenage daughter who had the upper hand of her father.

Mazzy scanned the quiet carriage. "This train is like a library."

"Reading books is hardly a bad thing."

She peered over a schoolboy's shoulder, saw a cartoon office lady, skirt and blouse torn, devoured by an octopus.

"Well," I added. "It depends on what you're reading."

Yamada lived on a hill behind the station. Expensive, prized land passed down by his wife's family. Between modern apartment blocks sat his traditional house, wooden shutters and paper screens, a raked gravel garden. Small pine trees had been set beside stepping stones that laid a path from the gate to the door, and we balanced our way across and rang the bell.

His daughter, Michiko, had just graduated from MIT, and welcomed us in with an American accent that lit up Mazzy's eyes. Within minutes they were wandering the house with his wife, Hitomi, a music teacher who was as adept with the violin as she was at recalling the intricate histories of dead composers.

After a tour of her home, Hitomi fluttered around the kitchen, chopping vegetables and checking steaming pots, while our daughters popped out to fetch dessert.

Yamada proposed a drink. "A toast."

We went through to his study. Rows of files, books and bottles. He had a whisky collection to rival any Scotsman, and had gathered single malts from specialist distilleries around the globe.

"A winner first," he said, sliding out a bottle. "The Suntory Hibiki. 30 years old."

Yamada unscrewed the lid for me to savour the aroma.

"Marzipan. Vanilla?"

"And apricot, ginger. You wouldn't know it was 43% proof."

I watched him carefully pour.

"This is what we do best. Take someone else's idea and improve it." He passed me the glass. "Well, what we used to do best."

"Shall I drink?"

"Let it sit for a while, admire the nose."

I hovered over the glass. Inhaled oak and juniper. I looked at Yamada, eyes closed over the bouquet, the enigmatic man who'd represented Japan at kendo, who knew more about cult life than cult members.

"I never really asked what got you into social psychology, this obsession with conformity."

"I'm real *inaka mono*." He smiled. "Country pumpkin."

"Bumpkin," I laughed. "Though pumpkin works."

"Bumpkin, yes."

"The outsider in the big city."

"Free from my hometown. Expectations."

"My brother says I was a born psychologist. Awkward. A watcher rather than a doer."

Yamada nodded. "Once you set yourself apart from the group, you see it for what it is. There was a moment when I was young." He clicked his fingers, searching for the word. "Epiphany."

"This sounds interesting."

"Whisky first."

We touched the drinks and toasted. "*Kampai*."

"To daughters."

Yamada sipped and appreciated in silence, savouring each mouthful, studying the dark gold in his glass.

I drank too, tasting a hint of marshmallow. "Stunning," I said, feeling like the amateur connoisseur.

"*Subarashii*," Yamada confirmed, taking another, reverential sip, before he looked up and talked.

"I lived with my grandparents. My father was working in Osaka, and my mother lived in Nagoya, running a clothes shop.

I was told they lived apart for business reasons, and ignorantly I believed them. Anyway, my granddad kept some animals. A typical small farm. I knew he'd fought in China, and been a prisoner of war in Siberia, but this was never talked about. Well, until junior high school. I came home and dumped my bag in the kitchen. He'd cut himself sawing wood, and was sitting at the table drinking a beer with his bandaged hand. He gave me a glass of milk and told me to do my homework. I sat down and he picked up my history textbook. We both read quietly, a peaceful country kitchen. Then. Then he started, mumbling, slapping the pages. '*Nani kore?* What is this? A fantasy?' I told him it was about Japan in the war. 'Lies,' he exploded. 'They teach you fairy tales?' I'd never seen him like this. I was terrified. He flipped through the book before slamming it on the floor."

Yamada shook his head and finished his drink. "Poor man." He opened the mini-freezer by his desk and scooped out more ice cubes. From a shelf he took down another pair of tumblers. "New whisky. New glasses."

He gave no introduction to the pedigree of the next bottle, thinking about the past in his head, not the aged malt.

"Did your grandfather tell you the truth?"

"Ten years later. I was on a break from university when he took me into the garage. He said, 'The nail that sticks out will be hammered down.' A Japanese proverb about following the crowd. But he added, 'Better to dent the hammer with your head than crouch with the nails.'"

Finally, his grandfather told him about fighting in Manchuria. Marching across China under the rising sun of the Emperor.

"His best friend was lucky. A sniper killed him instantly, and his body was sent back to Japan for a proper funeral. When a dead soldier couldn't be recovered, his friend would cut off the little finger and mail it to the family. It was the fingerless corpses, the normalcy of washing rice in a blood-red river, that my grandfather admitted was more terrifying than death."

Not until a week before he died could he share the experience, and only then with his grandson, not his wife or his daughters.

"He died in shame. His unit captured a group of Chinese soldiers. They came under fire from another platoon, and his commanding officer ordered him to execute them. If he'd disobeyed an order in front of the enemy, his superior officer would've shot him. Although he couldn't refuse the command of bayoneting the prisoners, he said that he'd die a criminal for committing a criminal act."

Yamada finished his third whisky and put his hand on the bottle. Then he paused, thought better of another drink to cloud the story.

"Not just my grandfather. He held everyone from the Emperor down to those who physically carried out the atrocities responsible."

I looked up from the ice bobbing in my glass, finished an expensive, award-winning whisky, and could barely recall its taste.

Yamada studied the woodblock print on the wall. A lake scene with falling snow, a boat punted to shore, the faces of the female passenger and the boatman turned away from the viewer.

Before we had the chance for any trite conclusion, the theories on following and leading, the blind conformer, we heard the front door open, the rustle of bags and coats, our daughters.

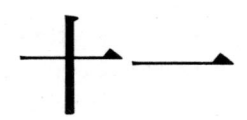

A WEEK AFTER starting his first job as a junior tax clerk, Koji rode the train back from his company dormitory and found his grandmother in the hallway. She'd been dead for three days. Her desiccated body no heavier than a pile of twigs.

Koji grabbed the phone to call someone.

Who?

He sat for a while on her favourite cushion. He expected her to move. To get up and shuffle into the kitchen and start cooking.

He studied the black and white wedding photo. Both his grandparents dressed in silk kimonos. His grandfather proud and stern, a hint of playing the samurai in the antique costume. His grandmother an ivory figurine, face white with heavy make up, her dark, painted lips.

Koji walked into the room he slept in as a boy. He stood before his father's portrait, the image his grandmother had honoured with burning incense. Koji hated his father's face, which had now become his face. He smashed the frame, took out the photo, and tore it into tiny pieces. He set fire to the fragments in a tea cup.

When Koji heard the gate shut, he knew who it was.

He slid back the screen and saw her on the path. His grandmother. Jabbing her walking stick before each step as though checking the firmness of the ground, whether it would take her eighty-nine years or not. She was going to the orchard to pick fruit from the laden boughs.

Koji watched her fade into the trees. She had once told him not to be afraid if he saw his grandfather's ghost.

All afternoon, Koji waited. A vigil. He hoped she might return with a bag of oranges to press into juice, vegetables to chop into a stew.

Finally he went downstairs and touched her hollow bones. Then he went outside, taking the dirt path that cut through a thicket of bamboo, between the shells of mangled cars and shattered glass. The same path he ran barefoot as a boy, before the lies of cities.

In the fields he saw men, farmers, knee deep in the flooded plains. As he walked he understood how each year the oranges swell with rain and sun, and then fall. How you can chart the progress of the stars on the reflection of a lake. How the wind ripples through shoots of rice like a wave does an ocean. The earth moved, he knew this much. Oblivious to the act played out upon its surface.

Koji stopped at the edge of the terraced fields, where the paddies gave way to mountains and myths. The boy in a peach and a girl from the moon, the lost princess. He took off his shoes and rolled up his trousers. He waded into the water, the soft mud between his toes.

十二

I LOVED MAZZY too much to be involved in her life. That was my greatest failure as her father.

Flying back to a frigid England from California, we hit some nasty turbulence over the Atlantic. The plane dipped and lurched, felt like a rickety glider put together with tape and glue. Cups and trays tumbled. People screamed, cried and vomited. The flight attendants sat with grim faced attempts at smiles while lightning cracked and blazed through the portholes.

Although I had no fear, I was well aware at how unhealthy, and selfish, this nihilism was.

I knew I had to get out of London when I had a fight on the tube. My first week back at work lecturing post-grad students on a rainy, February morning. Splashing down the escalators and cramming onto a carriage with the other sodden and miserable commuters.

There was an elbow in my ribs. I left it alone, stepped away. When the next rush of bodies hit the door I was pushed back onto the angry limb and prodded again.

We were wrestling on the lap of a shrieking woman before a Polish man and a builder hauled us apart. When I got a proper look at my opponent I saw he was in his late fifties, deep creases in a tired, life-beaten face. I shoved away the peacemakers and got off the train. In fear. Not at the aged opponent, but as if I'd just looked at the mask I'd grow into.

The memory of the Shikoku hitch-hike, the tunnel and the pearls, existed like a fairy tale kingdom. A Narnia that would reappear if I stepped again through the back of the wardrobe.

Or returned to Japan.

A month later, when news broke about a little known cult from Tokyo, the Pana-Wave Laboratory, attempting to net an Arctic seal strayed into a river, I saw the opportunity for another trip east.

Escape.

Pana-Wave members dressed in white to protect themselves from the electromagnetic radiation that communists, who were set on killing their leader, Chiho, a charismatic septuagenarian whose acolytes worshipped like a goddess, emanated from power lines. She believed the seal was confused by these evil rays, and that if they removed Tama-chan to the white-lined pool they'd constructed at their headquarters, before freeing her into the Arctic, the imminent May 15th doomsday would pass by harmlessly.

I talked the university into a research grant for Japanese cultism, a popular field since the sarin gas attacks by Aum Shinrikyo. Then I packed my life into cardboard boxes and drove out to a storage garage near Twickenham before a final pint in a pub by the Thames at Isleworth.

A day later I landed at Narita airport to be met by the tall and somewhat vampire-like appearance of Professor Yamada. Clad in black, with long dark hair falling down his cheeks, he was more Transylvanian fashion designer than fusty lecturer. And immediately likeable, a wide smile creasing around his sparkly eyes.

On the dashboard TV in his station wagon, we watched a live feed of the Pana-Wave convoy parked across a highway. Since failing to repatriate the strayed seal the group had been searching for refuge to ride out the impending devastation, when the Earth would pass by an invisible tenth planet of the solar system. This close encounter would switch the north and south poles, trigger tsunamis and quakes, and wipe out humankind.

Yamada pointed at the screen. "You see the swirls painted on the side of the trucks?"

"They diffuse evil rays."

He laughed. That deep, diaphragm bellow. "And you want to study this?"

I wasn't back in Narnia yet, but a return to the tranquillity of a Japanese lifestyle, despite being in the midst of a city twice the size of London, was the beginning of a recovery, a transformation.

Or simply forgetting. Living in a space that was free of Lydia memories. In Japan it was all me. My invention of a self. Friends and family were a mouse click away, but it's the day to day living that defines who we are, the bed we wake from, what's for breakfast, the angle of the sun, or lack of it, in the room you walk into when it's time to start work. The stock-taking hours of a lifespan.

I ate grilled fish and rice for breakfast. Bowls of miso soup. I kept my shoes clean because everyone else in the country did. I fell asleep with the audio files of my *Japanese for Busy People* textbook chattering in my dreams. I had stabs of self-awareness in the smallest things, the veins on a leaf that blew into a lift, the sound of rain striking a plastic bag.

Yet the back of that magical wardrobe couldn't be opened while I was boxed in a university office, collating data on Pana-Wave members' jobs, ages and occupations, and reading reports from their employers and teachers. Then a day before the predicted end of the world police raided Pana-Wave sites across Japan, including the camp atop Gotaishi mountain where Chiho lived in a van called Arcadia.

Born in Kyoto on the brink of World War II, Chiho was a baptised Christian who spent as much time at college as she did hospitalised from numerous suicide attempts. Accounts from her neighbourhood portrayed a woman who walked naked through the streets talking to the stars. Eventually she became a member of the now defunct God Light Association, and from the disbandment formed a breakaway sect combining Abrahamic ideology mixed with Buddhism, Hinduism and parapsychology. She also communicated with the dead, conversing with Pope John Paul II and Audrey Hepburn, as well as the rescuing aliens who were going to beam up the Pana-Wave believers from our doomed planet.

The white clad convoy was hounded by the media. There was a moral panic in the press and public who feared another Aum-like cult. Understandably, as the group had constructed a mobile laboratory and dressed as scientists. Initially I focused, entertained by the Sci-Fi doctrine – ET as angel, the flying saucers to save the faithful – and distracted from my own failings.

However, and not that unlike Pana-Wave members seeking escape from their daily lives, I needed an excursion beyond the Tokyo machine. A new fairy tale to lift me from the humdrum toil, the daughterless reality.

Instead of buying a ticket for a UFO I flew down to Fukuoka and saw old friends from my teaching stint, guys stranded in their ex-pat lives, some happily, some less so, realising that despite being married, having children and speaking fluent Japanese, they'd always be seen as foreigners, *gaijin*. We drank beer and ate Hakata ramen, talked about England with the wistful longing of men twice our age.

Then, rather than board the plane back to Tokyo, I took a train out to the northern highway and stuck out my thumb. I was too old for standing by the side of the road and waiting for a lift, but the destination was simply an excuse.

And I never even got past Hiroshima.

For hours I watched cars accelerate when they saw me, as if only hitting the ramp at maximum velocity ensured blast off and escape from the foreign hitcher. While trucks and buses rattled along the concrete bypass, I thought about Lydia, our final kiss outside the courthouse, the awkward hug. How she already saw me at some imagined distance.

Still waiting on the slip road when a thunderstorm burst over my head, I was soaked by the time two university students pulled over. They laughed hard at my bad Japanese and angled the heater vents onto my sodden jeans. After a short drive they dropped me outside Fukuoka where I bowed a thank you and pulled out my camera. I have a photo of them holding rolled up umbrellas like kendo swords. My plan was to photograph every driver who picked me up, a gallery of good Samaritans.

Next lift was a husband and wife, nurses who shared fruit

salad from a Tupperware box. They giggled and looked between the seatbacks, including the husband, jerking the car over the white lines each time we drifted towards oncoming traffic. My lens captured an odd moment, as they leant together and touched cheeks, giving the effect of conjoined twins merged at the face.

And then again a rainy highway, the swoosh of traffic on a wet road. Next hitch was an older couple and a similar photo, faces leaning in but not quite touching. Twins who'd survived the operation to separate one from the other.

I made it to Kita-Kyushu and hiked up a hill to the youth hostel, an empty box, divided into smaller boxes, containing empty bunk beds. No other guests. Going from room to room I didn't feel that I'd disturb a ghost, more that I actually was one.

I resisted the urge to call friends by doing some yoga and reading *Snow Country*, a Kawabata novel about a wealthy Tokyoite falling for a rural geisha. A lonely man living out a fantasy affair. Then I stared through a screen window on a city that wouldn't be here had it been sunny on the 11th of August 1945. Because cloud covered the Kita-Kyushu factories, the Enola Gay dropped the second atomic bomb on Nagasaki.

I dreamed of a flattened town. Wooden homes blown apart like models, the billowing mushroom. It was a startling vision to begin the morning with, and I slid from my sleeping bag and walked through an industrial estate, only looking for a lift when the weather bubbled and darkened.

The sky came down in waves, a downpour so torrential you could imagine koi swimming in the gutters. Once the rain ceased I hopped a barrier and climbed a steep verge to the highway. The sun burned itself through the clouds. Steam rose from puddles and wet grass. I sat on my pack and watched mountains emerge from misty valleys, temple roofs and factories, pylons striding across the hillside like hikers fixed on safety ropes. *Everything would be all right,* I thought. *Whatever happens.*

Then the Chief of Police for Foreign Crime pulled over and

picked me up. He told me his job when I asked how he'd learned to speak such fluent English.

"Interrogating drug runners and gangsters." He smiled. "Russians, Filipinos, Chinese and Americans. We all watch the same cop movies."

An hour later his stately Lexus deposited me on the melting tarmac of a Hiroshima pavement. I have a photo of the Chief posing before his car as though the proud owner of a new purchase. The moment he pulled away, a hot wind blew more rain from a bruise of clouds.

I was in *the* park, the site of the bomb. I sheltered from yet another storm with some tramps beneath a bandstand. They drank plum wine from jam jars. When a drain overflowed and flushed out a giant cockroach a barefoot drunk danced around it like a matador, his toothless fans cheering and calling for blood. He ran out of breath then speared it with the end of an umbrella.

And then the rain stopped. I splashed through puddles, watched clouds drift where sixty years ago the sky had ignited. Standing before the skeletal ruin of the one surviving building, the charred rafters jutting like the ribs of a body, I realised I couldn't face the tears and horror of the museum alone.

I'd already walked the bare hall in Nagasaki, seen children's paintings of exploding suns, fisted scrawls in red and orange. The matchstick families burning up in crayon.

After the park I felt empty. *Bereft* is the word I want to use, but of what I'm not sure. I have film-clip memories of a covered shopping street, a restaurant with plastic seats. Then a walled garden, temples and limpid pools. Along a gravel path between tiny, manicured trees, I met a German tourist, also hefting a backpack. He told me his name, but I don't care I've forgotten. I remember he was a scientist. Maybe genetics? Definitely a cold, exact subject. Together we climbed the pagoda and looked out over the city. The German suggested I get the bus with him to the youth hostel.

I said, "They close early."

He said, "There's nothing to do in Hiroshima after nine o'clock."

Then I just left, no polite excuses. I hated him for having the sense to eat and go to bed. I walked into a phone box and called Phil, an old teaching friend living in Matsuyama. No one picked up, so I called my mother in England. I'm not even sure why, and was glad when she didn't answer.

Next I walked into a bar I didn't leave until 6am.

It was a small, narrow room. The wooden walls lined with records. I sat on a high stool at the counter and drank a couple of beers before starting clumsy conversations with the other early birds, mostly scruffy, long haired drop outs of the Great Salaryman Race. My pocket dictionary and limited slang was all I had to patch together some banter. A guy with a ponytail and goatee told me he'd just come out of prison. When I asked, "For what crime?" he replied, "The whole world's a prison." But I may have misunderstood.

Once the words ran out I performed some tricks, coins vanishing, reappearing, a pepper pot smashed in a beer towel then found whole in a handbag. They liked that one, the crowd gathered at the bar and buying me drinks, having me buy them drinks.

And then everything changed.

She was sitting alone in the corner, smoking and drinking. She wore a turquoise Chinese dress cut to the top of her thigh. Her long hair was plaited into a single braid that hung down her chest like black rope. I was helpless. All teenage hormone, current and volts. As far from that measured and logical psychologist as I could possibly imagine.

Between thinking about speaking to her, and one more beer of courage, she left. Her chair and glass emptied. The warm glow of drinking with people whose names I didn't know turned to a tightness in my chest, panic.

I put down my beer, hurried outside, and apologised for following her onto the street. Then I asked if I could buy her a drink.

**

I took Mazzy on trips to museums and galleries, ambled around the tourist spots in Nippori and Ginza. We ate *mochi* cooked on glowing coals, sweet *anko* bean cakes shaped like fish. She made an effort for me, most of the time. Perhaps she felt sorry at my attempts to get her to like Tokyo, her father. She was happiest walking Michiko's Labrador in Yoyogi Park, watching the performance artists sing and dance. Tokyo, young and loud. Hip, if her generation even use that phrase. And chatting to Michiko at a thousand words per minute. I left them to it, walked beneath the crows that swirled above Meiji shrine and over to the international book store in Shinjuku, soothing my ego by confirming that *Gangs, Groups and Belonging* was stocked on the Kinokuniya shelves.

Then the brief holiday was over, and it was time for Mazzy to return to her studies. Yamada drove us out to The American School campus at Chofu. She was pretending to be nonplussed about the whole thing, but the disinterest wasn't convincing. She was looking forward to a new school, new friends. I'd already met with the gleaming Principle and been shown around the gleaming classrooms and the gleaming gym and met with some of the gleaming students. And the price of a semester matched the sparkle of the school.

"Did you check out their tennis courts?"

"All weather. The coach was ranked in the top hundred. A French guy."

I turned to her in the back-seat, tapping away at her screen.

"Don't pull out your phone in class."

"Jesus, dad."

"I'm just saying."

"What if my laces come undone? What should I do then?"

I saw Yamada holding back a smile, and I gave her no more advice on how to be a student. Not after she reminded me that she topped most of her classes in San Diego. Instead I waited until we pulled up, wished her good luck and kissed her on the cheek, and then watched her walk through the gates.

When I got back in the car, Yamada told me I should be proud. "She's smart. Mature."

"I'm adjusting to the fact."

"Michiko went to the US a girl, and came back a woman."

"A woman," I repeated. "That's a euphemism I don't want to think about."

I watched Mazzy till she disappeared through the school doors. She didn't turn to wave. She didn't need to.

"Let's take a walk," suggested Yamada. "Stretch our legs."

We drove towards Tokyo Bay. More suspended highways. Rooftops filled with air conditioning units, the occasional forlorn smoker puffing beside a whirring fan. I saw into tiny apartments, a man in boxer shorts stirring a cup noodle, a woman in pink ear muffs ironing. Then beyond the city centre, sun and space, the sky streaked with furrows of cumulus. Nearer the bay factories and warehouses appeared. When the road arrowed at the glittering water we took an exit and spiralled down to a park raised from reclaimed land, clusters of fir trees and an empty sports pitch.

"Before the earthquake," began Yamada, "this would be filled with footballers and golfers."

"Looks like good refuge, nothing to fall on you."

"The ground liquefied. Vibrated to mud then reset. A football team might break through the crust."

We climbed out of the car. A public toilet, sunk and tilted on its foundations, was roped off. On the baize grass a father and daughter flew a kite.

"They're safe," said Yamada, before glancing at my size ten shoes. "Well, a heavy *gaijin* might fall through, but us Japanese will be okay."

He smiled, scrunched up his face. "Just kidding."

I studied the rows of apartments that lined the flyover. Breeze-block grey. Meshed and frosted glass for tiny windows. Hundreds of identi-flats stacked twenty floors high.

"Company accommodation," confirmed Yamada. "Part of the wage packet."

I saw each room in a flash. As if I could click open the building like a fridge door and note its contents, strip lights in poky rooms, flickering TV screens.

"Stop working," said Yamada. "Take a break."

"If you're observing me then you're working too."

"*Sou desu ne,*" he agreed, shaking his head.

In the car boot, next to a stack of books including Skinner, Hamilton and Jung, alongside various Japanese titles with their original sleeves covered in brown paper, was a bag of golf clubs and a black leather case.

"I'm okay on the green." I inspected a putter. "But watch your head when I'm driving."

"No golf today."

He clicked open the case and pulled out a large brown envelope. We walked into the middle of the football pitch where Yamada studied the blue sky and I watched for cracks to appear in the earth and swallow us whole. Finally he opened the flap and carefully slipped out a sheet of white paper folded into a series of triangles.

"Last year I came third."

It was an intricately folded plane. Gently, he inspected the glider for any flaws, explaining that the national championships were next month, and that his latest design had already beaten the previous Japan record. "Here." He reached into his pocket and gave me an old fashioned stopwatch.

He crouched, closed the plane into an arrow, and placed it between his thumb and forefinger. "Ready?"

I held up the timer.

Then he uncoiled, launching the missile to a height of fifty metres before the wings flared open. The stillness of the day, the white plane looping in slow wide circles. It was a work of art.

Yamada followed its course, one hand hooding his eyes against the glare, and the other hand raised, hovering, like a poised conductor. When the glider came to rest in a graceful landing on the soft grass, I clicked the stopwatch.

"Twenty five seconds."

"Exactly?"

"Point two."

Yamada squatted and inspected his plane.

"Is that good?"

He studied the folds for any damage. "Three seconds off the world record." He held the plane by its nose and brought the wings level with his eyes. "Outdoor times don't qualify."

I watched him lost in the dynamics of his design, jealous he had a pastime beyond academia, language.

"You try."

I folded back the wings and launched the plane. Again, we watched it bank in slow, wide circles, following like parents of a child on a first bike ride. Proud, palms out to catch a fall.

After a few more launches Yamada noted the adjustments he needed to make and we walked over to a vending machine for a canned coffee.

"What simple joy." I snapped open my tin. "I loved making planes as a kid, but nothing that advanced."

"Two years ago I was on a project that dropped gliders from space and tracked them falling to earth."

"That's a serious hobby."

"We all need Zen. Especially us. We spend so much time studying others, and ourselves, that we need an activity beyond conscious thought."

"I started dance classes this year."

Yamada laughed. "That's far more difficult than folding paper."

"Salsa and tango."

"*Sugoi*," he praised. "No time for theorising while following steps."

"Maybe that's why I'm terrible. I ruined so many ladies' shoes. But you're right, a focus on body is vital. Zen."

In California, I'd run. Almost every day. Driving out to nature reserves and national parks with maps of trails that petered off into rockfalls of shale. Trails through narrow canyons where the rattlesnakes shook their hollow bones like maracas.

"The gregarious hermit." That's what Lydia had called me. "You have an ego in a room of people, have to be the centre of attention, love being the centre of attention. Then the next day you shudder at a voice. Head to the hills and start running for your life."

She bought me a pair of trainers with a GPS pod that slotted into the sole so she could join me on my runs, a virtual jogging partner. Microchips that tracked calories burned and steps taken. I never took it from the packaging. Never needed a screen or a number to tell me how far I'd run or what energy I'd used. Fatigue and sweat were the measure of toil and effort. A bounding mind when my body was finished.

But after the day at the beach, the wave, I lost the ability to switch off, and would run the dusty creaks thinking of rushing water, Mazzy.

"You're right," I said to Yamada. "I should keep dancing."

**

People danced. Did we? I can see her dancing and laughing, but this could be imagined.

Her name was Kozue. She told me that the kanji reads *Beauty dies young.* She was a hostess, but it wasn't a hostess bar, and I wasn't the kind of man who went to them. Besides, for each drink I bought her she bought me one back. I have no idea what we talked about, and the room filled with happy faces.

One man I saw made me think I should be a writer, a skinny guy on his own in the corner, probably English, inventing his own evening between the lines of an exercise book. An evening that he could fold away whenever he wanted. I had no choice. It was the evening that could fold me away.

Finally the bar quietened, just stragglers hunched over empty glasses. It was still light outside and I asked Kozue what time the sun set.

"That's the sun *rising*."

I wondered if I'd ever sleep again. At some point the barman had changed into a barwoman. "This not hotel," she warned, seeing my backpack.

We walked deserted streets. Objects blurred as though refracted through water. The office blocks fuzzed and wobbled as if Hiroshima had been submerged by melting icecaps and we were a mile under the sea. I wasn't afraid that my sight had gone, only that I'd stumble and be left on the kerb while Kozue swam away like a mermaid.

But we made it to her car, a blue jeep that complemented her turquoise dress. On the drive home she ran every red light. No traffic to stop for in a flooded city.

She lived on the top floor of an apartment set back in the mountains. I followed her swaying hips up a concrete staircase, that satin dress. With a coffee my focus returned, and I wondered if I'd tricked myself into how stunning she was, that the glare of day would reveal flaws, imperfection. I studied her heart-shaped face in the rising sun. The radiance of her skin, dawn flaring in the dark of her pupils. And her black, voluminous hair, spilling over her shoulders when she released it from the braid.

I woke up on the floor, with Kozue curled on the sofa. After I fell unconscious she must have draped a duvet over me and placed a cushion under my head.

I listened to her soft breath in the quiet room. She slept with the peace of a storybook maiden, and I walked around her apartment picking up things to check they were real. That I was. A pair of chrome chopsticks in a velvet case. Tea cups and earrings, a pot-pourri of cosmetics and creams. Her dress, hanging from the back of her bedroom door. I looked at the paintings on her wall. Mountains and rivers. Plaintive, wintered scenes. I swore I'd seen figures in the pictures before closing my eyes, men and women running and dancing, hunting in a forest. But I couldn't find them now, as if they'd climbed out of the frames during our sleep.

Kozue woke to the sound of me placing a glass of water on the coffee table.

"*Ohayo.*"

Delicately, she put the glass to her lips before leaning forward and kissing me softly on the cheek. Neither of us were surprised to find ourselves together. With a silky black gown clinging to her body she walked over to the stereo, slid a record from a sleeve and placed it on the turntable. "Do you know this?"

A hiss and crackle, before the haunting bars of Terence Trent D'Arby's *Sign Your Name* cut my soul from my body. I hovered just below the ceiling. Hearing a song I obsessively listened to as a student while wondering about women and love, I actually felt sick with the force of being alive. I had to run outside because I thought I'd vomit. But nothing. My stomach would flutter like this for weeks, months, every time I thought of her.

From the balcony I found the grainy outline of Hiroshima through the clouds. In fear of falling, I gripped the rail so hard I could see the whites of my knuckles. When I looked back into her room she was putting on make up in the mirror, painting her face with all the focus of an artist before a dappled landscape.

Of course, the pictures on the wall were hers.

There was nothing more to be done.

I went inside and we kissed. A honeyed sweetness to her lips. I undid her gown and let it fall from her shoulders. She stood in the sunlight, completely at ease with her nakedness. Softly I kissed her neck and her breasts before kneeling on the wooden floor.

I wish I could recall more about our first conversations, but I have little memory of what we actually spoke about.

I know we drove out to the beach in her blue jeep, and that I sang *Light My Fire* when she asked if I liked karaoke. Then passing a hotel I thought I'd misunderstood everything. She pointed and said, "I use these rooms with my clients."

A prostitute? I knew hostesses who did more than serve drinks and giggle to make lonely salarymen feel wanted. But she wasn't a woman who sold her body by the hour. She told me the hotel was where she worked a second job, dressing brides and arranging hair on wedding mornings. Was I relieved, or somehow disappointed? The fact is I didn't care if she was a prostitute.

At the beach we followed a path beneath cliffs and overhanging trees that grew from solid rock. I took her hand as we walked around a small bay. Clouds swelled, primed to rupture. But it wasn't fear of rain that made us turn back.

Sitting, perched over us like a gargoyle, was a cat. The scrawniest, ugliest cat I've ever seen. Hissing and spitting with bared fangs and spiked hackles, as if some creature drowned by the sea and then spat ashore to claw my eyes out. We backed away, and then fled to the jeep, glad to be chased by the falling rain, and not the cat.

Kozue accelerated from the storm and drove to the mouth of a river. First we sat, dangling our legs over the harbour wall. Then she laid down with her head in my lap. I trailed my fingers over her bare shoulders, through her glossy hair. When I slid my hand up her dress she closed her eyes and gripped my wrist.

By the time we came up for air the sun was setting as though the clouds were on fire.

**

On the drive back from the park with Yamada, we slipped into a relaxed silence. In Japan one can sit in a meeting and say nothing following a question. Better to consider the thought than fill the void with waffle.

But I'm not Japanese.

"You're right about a hobby," I began. "I've been buried in work, books and words. All mind. Watching the human subject, the rat in a box, not a kindred spirit, soul, however you want to define a self."

"I'm surprised to hear you use the word soul."

"Consciousness."

"Defined by a god?"

"If I use soul?"

Yamada turned down the concerto for a discussion, a confession.

I said, "This is embarrassing, but when I got to university I still believed in God. Not a god. God. Our Heavenly Father, all that business. I never took the bible seriously, but I had some vague image of a man with a white beard hovering around the ether."

"A God without a church, a doctrine?"

"I suppose so. But He was there. I was sure of it. I saw messages in leaves blown by the wind. A white horse in a field. I prayed. Crazy."

"Not crazy," said Yamada. "Human."

"Then I read books, travelled. Revelations from science and knowledge, that our bones are made of blown up stars. I understood atoms and time. How the dragon legend came from a dinosaur skeleton. One mystery had been solved, but the stark cold truth was terrifying. A blankness."

"But still the mystery of people."

"Yes," I said. "*Yes*."

Yamada nodded. Then he said nothing. We drove for half an hour in silence, up and down the elevated highways, past concrete rivers and faceless towers.

I thought of Kozue and her slender fingers, how she liked to press her palm against mine.

I was still thinking of her when Yamada began a careful speech on Christianity and guilt, theorising that Japanese soldiers were capable of such cruelty during the war because they had no supernatural judgement of their actions. No watching overlord.

"Apart from their commanding officer. Ready with a gun should they disobey."

He nodded to himself, continued with the theme as he drove, contradicting himself when he talked of a divine Emperor.

But I was too distracted for a riposte.

I pictured her on the bed, reaching over to grab a hairbrush. The cat-like arch to her back.

"And sex," I thought aloud. "No one watching."

Yamada looked across. "God is in bed with you?"

"Even when you don't believe, it's hard to de-program the idea."

He thought about this, stroking his Confucian chin. "My mother and father are part of my self, who I am. Of course not ghosts or floating spirits, though definitely a presence. But I don't think dead ancestors follow their children into a love hotel."

**

A year after the Hiroshima hitch-hike, in a bland hotel on the M25, I told Lydia about Kozue.

She'd flown Mazzy over to stay with me for a month. She stood and stared from a 6th floor window overlooking a car park, talking logistics, what time I'd make certain phone calls, bedtimes and diet. Then she turned and promoted the new man her in her life. "A good man," she assured. "Older. Great with Mazzy."

I looked at Mazzy asleep on the armchair, curled around a bobbled teddy bear, thumb in her mouth.

Instead of hating the substitute father, the stranger picking up my daughter and carrying her to bed, I described the colour of Kozue's jeep, details of sky and sea. The deja vu of waking in her Hiroshima apartment. The deja vu of right there, Lydia, standing in a hotel room as planes roared overhead.

She'd listened, I think, while I talked.

Then she said, "How am I supposed to compete with this? We meet on the driveway of a self-induced massacre, hate the sight of each other, and then grudgingly start dating two months later."

I told her, "No."

I told her I'd die with the memory of us trespassing in the nature reserve, walking the trails naked. The Yellowstone cabin heaped with snow, kissing in a frozen forest. Sex during a squall in her uncle's beach house, the world beyond the rattling window destroyed by thunder and lightning as we fastened our bodies tighter and tighter together.

Our daughter.

But she'd had enough of us, me. The person she had to regress into whenever we met. Mazzy would wake to find her mother gone, back to California aboard one of the planes that juddered the hotel room. She cried non-stop for two days, and then forgot her parents when my sister-in-law put a Husky puppy in her arms.

Lydia had rung, often. Beyond the agreed timetable of transatlantic telephone calls. She was missing Mazzy, the first time she'd been in a different country to her daughter. The first time she'd been entrusted solely into my care. She said I shouldn't have told her about Kozue, but she understood that I had to redefine my masculinity, to push a new self into a family dynamic from which I was fading.

"But don't think I wanted to hear that. I gave you scant details of Per because you can't handle a reality not on your terms."

"Per," I said, petulantly. "Has he got a Viking longboat in the garage?"

"Jesus, Ben."

I'd rarely asked about her exes, riling her that I was erasing the past by not wanting the details of her previous lovers.

I doubt she wanted to know how Kozue drove me to an Italian restaurant where I sat stupefied as the alcohol in my veins turned to glue. The hangover had arrived. My stomach felt like a deflated balloon. I forced down a few bites of pizza, but we had to leave before my body turned itself inside out.

When I realised I'd forgotten my Japanese dictionary in the

bar, I was happy. Not because it meant communication had to be in English, but for a sense of purpose. We could drive back to the bar and pick it up. Maybe have a drink, or two.

It was as busy as the previous night, but without the friendly buzz. Or is this all bars when you walk in sober? Tonight the bar*woman* was the bar*man*, and either he was unimpressed that I was back so soon, or that I was escorting Kozue. I sat at the same stool I'd done the night before, and with my first beer I extinguished all the daylight between my last drink that very morning.

Then *He* walked into the bar.

Even before he'd leant in my face and hissed something in Japanese, I knew he was her boyfriend. I asked Kozue what he'd said, who was he? She shook her head and mumbled something I didn't catch.

He seemed to know everyone in the room, greeting the other men with solemn nods. This night I was the only *gaijin*. The escapade had turned into a trap. Kozue had said nothing about a boyfriend, and a jilted man sat plotting my death, shamed before his peers, while I bought his girlfriend drinks.

It was no surprise when I was dragged off the barstool. I made sure he came to the floor with me, punching, scratching and gouging all the way down. If this were England his friends would've been kicking at me like a dog. But this was Japan, where the valour of the samurai lives on in salarymen and students, the cheated boyfriends. We scrabbled one on one, left to brawl before a ring of his mates. Only when I levered enough space from his grip to start swinging my elbow did the barman hurdle the counter and break us up. I could hear Kozue shouting as I was garrotted to my feet.

When the barman thrust the Japanese-English dictionary into my hand it felt like a visa I could brandish at the blocked doorway.

Finally I was beyond the melee, bundled from a fire exit. My neck burned, sliced where my collar had cut the skin. And Kozue was with me, clutching my hand and apologising.

"It's my fault," I told her, skittering down the metal staircase.

But after a day and night together she'd run away with me, not him. And whatever it was that we were doing, it was a palpable rush.

However, my booming heart stopped when he leant over the rails and barked her name, roaring at the night like an ogre in a tower, the fair maiden freed by the dashing prince. Though I doubt he saw things this way.

We didn't run. The three of us stood on the forecourt of a derelict garage in a dim lit back street, behind the air-conditioning units of a pachinko parlour blowing out stale cigarette smoke. Neon signs from poky izakayas melted onto the surface of oily puddles. It was the kind of film noir scene where the good guy lies slumped with a knife in his side, blood thinning in the rain.

But who was the good guy?

They spoke low, measured sentences, punctuated by curses and insults. If I'd had my bag I would've walked away there and then. This was nothing to do with me. That was what I kept telling myself. Even though it was all to do with me, and her, and him.

He was twitchy, right in her face. I stood between them, my fist clenched. They argued some more, and I understood little. I said a few things in Japanese, that I didn't know about any of this. Then we all shoved each other and he just left, storming back to the bar. When Kozue said, "Let's go," I needed no encouragement.

She drove back to her apartment. I walked in behind her, straight to my bag. Kozue grabbed the handle. "You can stay here, this is my home, not his."

I wasn't waiting for him to roll up with a carload of friends, and I told her this. She shook her head. "He is not my husband. We are not together. I am I. He is he, and you are you."

The list of pronouns was infallible, but I still called her a liar.

"You never even asked if I had a boyfriend."

I pulled my bag from her grip and walked out the door, a gesture of leaving that I had to follow through with, even though I didn't want to go.

I hiked towards the glow of Hiroshima, emotionally and physically shattered. Just as I'd decided to unroll my sleeping mat in a bamboo thicket, headlights swung my shadow across the verge.

**

Tokyo has a history of bad dreams. Most of the minor tremors, the rattling windows and tinkling pots, the creaking walls and opening doors, occur at night. The city stirs like a child or cat twitching in its sleep, and the tectonic plates gently rock the hard earned slumber of the metropolis without commotion, before it closes its eyes again.

On arrival at Redwood Towers I was shown around by the concierge, a man as obsequious as he was bureaucratic, and handed a welcome DVD which included details on the laundry service, garbage disposal, and a short clip of a scale model of the building wobbling on a quake simulator. After a lab coat presenter switches off the machine, he explains how the architecture has been designed to sway and shift on the seismic energy, and that any movement, particularly on the upper floors, was nothing to be concerned about.

I still recall my first quake. Like a presence in an empty room. I was sitting in an old wooden house on my first trip to Tokyo. I called out because it was a flimsy build and usually when the walls shivered it was because someone was walking up the staircase. But no one answered. And then the CDs flopped against one another and the plates in the sink tinkled musically and the chair I was sitting on inched across the floor. It was the swinging lampshade that confirmed the tremor, and my cowardice, when confronted by the whim of a molten planet patched together with the odds and ends of broken stars.

When the first serious tremor shook my apartment, Mazzy was in her room, tapping away on her iPad.

"Dad?"

She felt the judder a second before I did, and ran into the kitchen.

"Don't panic."

"I feel sea sick."

The walls creaked and shifted. As if the whole building were flexing in the breeze.

"It'll be over in moment."

"Dad."

Mazzy grabbed my arm tight, and hugged me.

I never thought I'd be glad to feel an earthquake, but when she found comfort in her father I was happy that one tectonic plate was bumping another.

Finally the vibrations stopped, and once the bricks and mortar had settled Mazzy let go and put on a brave face.

"I've had worse in LA."

"Don't tempt fate."

"Fate, said the scientist."

She marched back to her room and I asked if she was okay.

"Cool. I'm gonna tweet it."

I stood in the middle of the kitchen, certain the apartment was still moving.

Yamada had thought the Tohoku quake was *The One*, the catastrophic subduction of the Pacific and Eurasian plates that Tokyoites are quietly and stoically expecting.

"I was on the top floor of Building 8 at the Komaba campus," he told me. "On the very first jolt the tower actually jumped. No warning tremor or vibrating desk, just a boom of force."

Roof tiles loosed from the ceiling and shattered on the floor. Yamada saw his department head crying beneath a table. Computers rocked then dropped. Screens exploded. Everything shunted from left to right, drawers shot open and ejected themselves from filing cabinets. The block swayed back and forth for minutes, and Yamada had felt like a cricket clinging to a reed.

"And this was hundreds of kilometres from the epicentre. We filed downstairs into the lobby. We were supposed to go to the evacuation zone, but some of us stayed and watched the TV in the canteen. The terrible silence when we saw the helicopter above the wave."

I was still thinking of Yamada when I sat back at my desk. Even the squeak of my wheelie chair made me nervous. "Shall we get a coffee?" I called to Mazzy.

"From the cafe?"

"Sure."

I wanted to be on the street, outside. I put my shoes on and stood by the door. When Mazzy dipped back into her room for her phone I stepped onto the landing.

I had no reason to be shocked by a man standing there, but I was spooked by the quake and it was rare to see any of my neighbours. It was the measured way he turned and studied me, his immaculate suit and polished shoes. Not a strand of his thick black hair out of place. He simply nodded once and took the staircase instead of waiting for the lift.

Then a flashback. Something familiar.

That cauterised gaze.

I thought of the Pana-Wave ranks on Gotaishi mountain. Masquerading as a journalist, I'd been escorted through the bandaged trees by lab coated peons. In a clearing covered with sheets, I was beckoned to sit before Chiho and her retinue of followers. Their hanging faces, incredulous at my questions. Glaring through Cheshire cat smiles as I challenged her cod philosophy. She was the wrinkled Buddha, commanding the crowd with a glance or a word, her absolute faith in delusion.

Admittedly, I too had been one of the intrigued. But after a second doomsday passed without UFOs or catastrophe, the press lost interest, along with numerous Pana-Wave members despite Chiho's claims that the earth had been saved at her command.

I concluded my research with a well-received paper on 'How prophets reign over a kingdom of unprovable truth,' and continued reading her updates, long, rambling messages about the spaceship they were constructing and how Japan would sink to the bottom of the sea. With fascination and horror, I followed the group's decline. The preparation of a launch pad, the failed alien visit when dozens of spaceships crashed into the Pacific. And the police investigation of a runaway girl who vanished from the group, and then seemingly the world, as if benevolent aliens really had beamed her up.

Nearly ten years since I caught the old woman's stare, her black eyes cutting like obsidian. Yet she remained in my psyche, beyond her death, and Pana-Wave's ultimate disbandment.

I called into the apartment and asked Mazzy why she needed her phone every second of the day. Then I opened the staircase door and listened for his footsteps. Nothing. I peered from the window down to the entrance. He never did emerge.

十三

WHEN THE EARTHQUAKE struck Koji was in the coffee shop outside her apartment. Waiting. Then inside her apartment. He wanted to assure her that the tremor had been caused by the great catfish that lives beneath the city, and that when it thrashes its tail, Tokyo shudders. He wanted to explain that the stone pillar at Kashima shrine goes to the centre of the world, and that as long as it holds down the catfish's head, she was safe.

Instead her father had seen him.

Studied him.

As if he knew something.

Nothing.

He knew more about his daughter than he did. He was the one who watched her home from school. The one who followed her around the shopping arcades.

It didn't matter that her father was incapable of looking after her, because he'd taken care of women before.

Despite what The Leader believed.

In a room with white sheets hung over the windows, white sheets draped over the chairs, they had told him to leave. The Leader had been wheeled into the room wearing her white yukata. She told Koji that it wasn't her decision, nor any other individual passing judgement.

It had spoken.

It, the ethereal consensus.

Koji had acted as an individual, she accused. Not as part of the group. He'd driven to Mount Fuji with one of the new recruits, a student drop-out from a fishing village in Hokkaido. She was a girl with tracks of scars along her wrists. She wouldn't eat for days. Together, they'd walked into The Aokigahara Sea of Trees.

The suicide forest. In the damp undergrowth, where mushrooms sprouted in the mossy dells, and the lava bed floor was strewn with fallen trunks, they looked for bodies. Koji told her that if she died here she'd be taken into the soul of the mountain and live forever.

He showed her the green bones of a man who'd taken an overdose. Or cut his wrist. Who could tell. The body had been there a long time, outlasted by the remains of a silk tie. She asked Koji if the man was free, and Koji said he was. Then she walked along the dark path in front of him, a delicate girl, weak, treading feebly. The trail was littered with fist-size lumps of volcanic rock.

She was free.

That was what Koji told The Leader.

When she told him to leave, it felt like death. Or how the world was before he met her, the withered old lady who'd found him on a park bench a week after his grandmother's funeral. She'd sat down and began whispering to herself. Another senile pensioner wandering the streets, thought Koji. He ignored her, finished his bento and went back to his office. The next day he went to the park as usual, feeding stray cats slivers of fish, shooing away the crows. Again, she appeared and sat down beside him. This time she said, "*Konnichiwa*," and he caught her eyes. Lit points of black in a white face. Sparkling dark. As if she'd trapped the soul of a high school girl in her decaying body.

She told him that it didn't matter he had no family, or that he was the last one, because a new family was waiting for him.

十四

DAWN ON HIROSHIMA docks. A security guard knocked on the jeep windscreen. Kozue had fallen asleep with her dress around her waist, and the elderly official stared at her breasts. She lifted the straps onto her shoulders, and parked outside the ferry gates.

After Kozue had picked me up from the bamboo thicket we'd driven down to the seafront, hugged, kissed and slept. Unsure of whose life I'd walked into, and the man I'd upset by doing so, I told Kozue I was going to Shikoku to see Phil, and that I'd be back in a couple of days.

"I need to breathe," I told her. "Think."

It was simply a pause from my hitch-hike to Tokyo. I could talk myself back to reality. Well, that was the neat logic.

"Don't lie to me," she'd warned. "Say nothing, or tell the truth if you're running away."

Rather than the ferry pulling away from the port, the port seemed to pull away from the ferry, breaking off the hull and floating the tide. Kozue stood by her jeep and watched. She waved, just once. Beneath the overcast morning, sky and sea were the same shade of mercury. I went inside and bought a rice ball wrapped in seaweed, took one bite, and threw the rest over the rail.

Trams rattled streets below the ramparts of a reproduction castle. Phil was still at work, and I fell asleep in a park where schoolboys pinged baseballs into the tops of trees, flushing pigeons from the boughs.

An hour later, limbs stiff and kidney aching, I met Phil and caught the tram back to his place. He knew I'd messed up the moment he saw my face. His girlfriend knew, too. Ayumi had moved into his apartment and turned it from a hovel to a home. She made tea and smiled. But in their little house I was a straggly dog come in from the rain. When I confessed the story of Hiroshima I felt like I'd shaken my dirty pelt across their spotless living room. They both guessed what I didn't want to think, that Kozue was some kind of yakuza girl.

"She paints," I said, as if that were enough to prove she wasn't mob affiliated.

After a night on their floor, all of us essentially in the same room with only a paper screen dividing us, the two of them did the thing that proper people do and went to work, while I tramped around Matsuyama.

I hiked up to the castle and patrolled the sun-bleached watchtowers. Eyeing the town through the slits, I imagined myself an archer loosing arrows at marauding invaders, tipping out pots of boiling tar and launching spears down the slopes. First the attackers were raging barbarians, all spit and snarl with feral beards, falling from ladders and the ends of swords, stumbling before rolling bales of flaming hay. But then the enemy had a face, the boyfriend. My arrows thudded into his chest, two between his ribs, the third and final through his neck. The princess saved, Kozue and the castle intact.

I was done for. Well and truly.

And so would he be if I went back to Hiroshima.

How beautiful the drab toil of a commute, work, and then returning to the one you love, had suddenly become. Phil and Ayumi woke, showered, dressed in clothes they had laid out the night before, and cooked extra rice for breakfast so they could take a boxed lunch to the office. At the end of the day they came home to each other and watched films, usually dramas or thrillers about other people's perils and mistakes.

I trudged back to the city and sat in a restaurant where the meal is free if you can eat 1.3 kg of curry and rice in twenty minutes.

I ate less than half and paid full-price.

Outside the midday sun hammered at the empty streets. Everyone was working. I walked into a phone box and rang the number Kozue had written on a utility bill, but got the answer machine. I put the phone down and left my hand on the receiver. Trams shook themselves along grooves in the road. Downtown glared, reflected off shop front windows. It was touching forty degrees in the shade, and the towers wobbled and shimmered as if the city was melting into a pool of glass and slag.

I picked up the phone and dialled. This time I left a message saying I'd be in Hiroshima that night.

For the first hour I hitch-hiked from the wrong junction, waiting on the slip road back to Matsuyama. Not that things got any better when I stood in the right spot.

After a few minutes at the entrance to the toll bridge a couple pulled over and asked if I was going to Hiroshima.

"*Hai, hai*," I answered. "*Hiroshima ni ikimasu.*" I got in the backseat hoping for a quiet ride across the channel.

They were Japanese Jehovah's Witnesses. In broken English, while watching my face in the rear-view mirror, they told me to offer my soul to God and pray for redemption.

The Seto-Ohashi road bridge is the longest in the world.

On the outskirts of Hiroshima I called Kozue, again. Still the answer machine. It was nine o'clock and I guessed she was already pouring drinks. I left a message that I'd wait for her beneath the fountain outside the Matsuya department store.

After a long night nervous of every shadow, she pulled up in her jeep as the sun rose. Her hair was tied back and she was a little drunk. We kissed. She tasted of rum. We said very little. Neither of us had slept, and I refused to go back to her apartment. We agreed to meet at midday, and for the next six hours I slept in the torpedo-sized chamber of a capsule hotel.

Then I woke, showered, and walked into Hiroshima.

Kozue had tickets for an exhibition of the photographer Robert Capa, and we met in front of the art museum. We walked in holding hands, and then separated inside the gallery, drawn from picture to picture at a different pace. There were fuzzy prints of the D-Day landings, the contentious image of the dying militiaman, either his arms flung back at the force of a bullet, or the director's command.

One photo we stood before together.

Vietnam. A soldier lies on his back in a shallow trench, and you know that above his head metal is searching for flesh. But this GI has found the eye of the storm. With the last of a cigarette pinched between his lips, he folds his arms and gazes into sky, beyond treetops and cloud, beyond war. Until he puts out his cigarette and sits up, nothing can touch him.

After the photo we walked around Hiroshima. I thought the hollow sensation was a feeling in my chest, but Kozue told me that sections of the city had been built on a river delta, and that if you lifted certain manhole covers you could look down onto the marsh below.

She worked two hostess jobs, and I was to meet her at midnight. I spent an hour in a fast-food place before I walked into a military apparel shop and bought a flick knife with a serrated blade.

Well, this was the fantasy I created while waiting. That I searched Hiroshima until I met the boyfriend, the man who'd held her delicate jaw in his hands, right in front of me, just to prove he could break it like glass.

Not that I needed to add a sense of drama, a duel with knives in a dead end street. Because truth writes its own narrative, is stranger than fiction.

**

Mazzy was over her jet-lag, sleeping a regular pattern, and even listening to her Japanese language CDs. School had invigorated her relationship with Japan, her father. She met up with Michiko and ate tempura, twice ventured out on her own, confident, she said, in the swirling crowds and circuit board map of the Metro. She caught the train to Harajuku, came back with new clothes and photos of Meiji shrine. I greeted her as if she were an intrepid explorer returning from the Amazon.

"You were the one who told mom it was the safest country in the world."

"Perhaps I was exaggerating."

"Earthquakes and tsunamis. Radiation. Yeah, just a little."

Photos had appeared from the first journalists who ventured into the Fukushima exclusion zone. Buildings ripped up by the wash of a wave, ghost foundations where houses had vanished. The ubiquitous boat on a roof, boat on a bridge. Boat run aground outside a supermarket. Beyond the reach of the brimming sea, but glowing with fallout from the broken reactors, lay the abandoned towns. The living rooms paused with cups of tea and opened newspapers: reports of a community sports day, petty crime and local politics, a discount coupon for a new shrimp restaurant.

We know time has passed because a bowl of rice has a coat of mould, the neat gardens astray with green. In a shopping arcade grass shoots up from the steps of an escalator. How quickly the earth reclaims its space from our feeble endeavours. Whether it be a quake shivered wave or a windblown seed.

The lead image was an escaped pig, fast asleep in the mess of a shop it had pillaged. No subtext was needed. It was a pig in a sweet shop.

I had an invitation from an NGO affiliated with the university to visit reconstruction efforts on the edge of the safe zone. Yamada explained how sports halls sheltering the refugees had been carefully organised, and such was the precision that street layouts had been taped onto the wooden floors, meaning that families huddled under sleeping bags were most likely previous neighbours. However, the close-knit spirit of these defiant fishing towns meant the families who left, the concerned parents worried about caesium in the playground, strontium in the sandpit and plutonium in the air conditioning, were being shunned for abandoning their community.

Natural catastrophes weren't my only concern.

I knew what Mazzy didn't know about the sects and cults. How an individual could drop from society and reinvent the world through a warped doctrine. Or perhaps more worrying, the loners who don't find the groups, the *otaku* who construct a life from manga and computer games, pornography. An altogether darker reality from the kitsch and cute public face of a very private country.

"Don't get nonchalant about your well-being," I told her more than once. "It's far safer than walking around London or LA, but the crazies here are better hidden."

"You told me never to use the word crazy."

"Crazies, is different. A noun, not a label."

She tutted, not unlike her father, before plugging in her headphones and walking out.

A minute later there was a knock at the door. No one ever knocked. If it was reception they rang or buzzed. And Mazzy knew the door was open. Unsettled, I got up and looked through the spyhole, half expecting it to be the young man wandering the lobby from the day before.

It was the obsequious concierge clutching a delivery.

"We have received a delivery for Monroe san."

"Thank you."

"You have identification?"

"You know it's me."

"Ah, sorry. Yes. Do you have ID card? Passport?"

He made the outline of a card with his thumb and forefinger, balancing the package between his elbows rather than simply passing it over.

"You've seen my passport. A dozen times."

"For identification reason."

I'd dealt with him on a regular basis, signed documents and printed forms with my *hanko,* a carved wooden stamp, specifically for the world of officialdom. But each time it was as if we'd never met. I looked at the package in his grip, pictured us wrestling to the floor and only prizing it from his lifeless hands.

I asked him to wait a moment, "*Chotto matte kudasai*," continuing with our ridiculous game of him insisting on speaking to me in English, even when I replied in Japanese.

I grabbed my passport and gave it to him.

"Thank you so muchee." He checked the photo and the information page, bowed far too deeply for the transaction of a parcel, and backed away.

I took the box inside and set it on the table. I hadn't ordered anything, but there was my name on the label. With a knife I slit the tape and pulled out the bubble wrapped contents. A bright orange device, a hybrid design between a TV remote and a ray gun. I peeled off the cellophane and read the attached bumph.

The Gamma-Scout is a general purpose survey meter that measures alpha, beta, gamma and x-ray radiation. It has proven to be useful in the medical, nuclear, mining, metal scrap and foundry industries. It is also used by first responders, police, customs and border control, hobbyists, rock hounds and in personal or home survival kits. The Gamma-Scout sets a new standard in portable geiger counter performance and functionality.

Gracias. Lydia.

I looked again at the outer packaging and realised the addressee was only Mazzy, 'Courtesy of Ben Monroe,' as if I were a body indifferent to radiation. I was tempted to bin the bloody thing rather than have a paranoia contraption lying around, but Lydia would no doubt be asking after its safe arrival.

I was still reading the instructions when Mazzy came back from her run, perspiring, breathing hard.

"Shoes."

"They're not dirty."

She had one foot on the polished wooden hallway.

"It's bad karma."

"You don't believe in karma."

"Something like that."

She backtracked and unlaced, saw the opened box. "What's the present?"

"From your mother."

Mazzy knelt down by the coffee table and picked up the Gamma-Scout, punching buttons and turning it over in her hand.

I read, *"The Gamma-Scout geiger counter has a large digital screen that can display the radiation detected as dose rate or in pulses – total count or per second. There is also a logarithmic bar chart to quickly visualize the magnitude of the measured dose rate. Additional visual indicators show if monthly or annual dose thresholds have been exceeded."*

"Holy crap, mom." Mazzy aimed at me and pretended to shoot. "Have you got some batteries?"

"No, luckily."

"We might be glowing and not even know it."

"Breathing LA smog is far more lethal than a hyped Tokyo fallout."

"Still, it's nice of her to send it over."

Nice? A Trojan fucking horse, that's what it was. Lydia was on the other side of the Pacific, yet here she was in the room, chiding the father of her only daughter for not taking proper care of her darling.

**

I met Kozue in Hiroshima at midnight. She wore a loose, black dress, with a swooping cut that revealed her pale shoulders. We sat at the counter in an *okonomiyaki* restaurant, watching chefs chop, dice, and fry pancakes on a greasy skillet. I ate everything that we ordered, concentrating on the food with a steely determination.

Then we walked into the slick, humid air. From machine cool to musty dark. When a rabble of boys skateboarded past I thrust out a defensive elbow, catching a floppy-haired teen who swerved too close. Kozue gripped my hand that bit harder. Finally I asked more about what she did, who she was. What was her relationship with the man who'd garotted me from the barstool.

"Why are you talking about something that has gone?"

She was annoyed by my dumb rhetoric, a hint of anger.

"Yesterday is hardly ancient history."

"Do you know the name of the soldier in photo?"

The GI in the trench, the relentless moment.

"No idea."

"What are you doing?"

"Right now?"

She held out her palms in exasperation. "Where else is now?"

"Walking with you."

"So?"

We left the busy shopping street and I followed Kozue into a small park alongside the river. We stood by a rail and looked into the pond at the foot of a miniature waterfall. Fat koi bumped and nudged one another, gaped at the air.

I had a thousand questions about hostessing, the fine line between selling a body by the hour and a once revered art form. Instead I put my hand on the small of her back, leaned over and kissed her neck.

We walked into the basement lobby of a love hotel and chose a room from the illuminated display. A sunken bath, mirrors. A huge, circular bed, and plush carpets that sank with each footstep.

I looped my hands around her waist and pulled her tight, grabbing her hips.

She looked past my shoulder to the bathroom, and told me to wait. She shut the door and locked it. I heard running water. Steam seeped out from around the frame, and when finally she opened the door again she was naked, her hair pinned up.

Then she stepped forward and unbuttoned my shirt, hanging it carefully on the rail before undoing my belt. I slipped off my clothes and she took my hand, leading us into the bath.

I had two texts from her the following month. And one phone call, the day after the night in the hotel. After I'd been fired back to Tokyo on the bullet train. In the morning she'd asked me if I knew what I'd done. I said I was confused. Even though I knew full well what she meant, because my body was thrumming. I'd woken up as if I hadn't recognised my own skin, before she kissed me on the cheek and vanished out of the door, apologising.

My concentration was shot. I had to delay my trip to the Pana-Wave camp in Gotaishi Mountain, wholly unprepared for the scoop meeting with Chiho in her mobile headquarters. It was an academic coup, raw data from a sect leader at the height of her nefarious powers.

But another woman was calling.

Commuting to work, standing in the shower or lying in bed. I spoke her name, felt the shape of it in my mouth, the weight of her on my tongue. I could barely see beyond her face, the slender fingers, her hands pressed against mine. Each thought was a superficial front to reality. My world was not a packed train to an office. Not a screen filled with data on cult members in fear of electromagnetic waves, the Earth flipping its poles.

The recurring image of her looking back into her apartment, seeing the care and precision in which she applied her make up.

How she walked in the hotel corridor, the poise of her steps, the black dress slipping down her pale arms, and the thin gold chain around her wrist.

I rang her from Tokyo four or five times. No answer. I was desperate, I acknowledged that much. Yes, I'd jumped the dulled state following the divorce, losing Mazzy, but if I were the psychiatrist analysing my self from a separate couch I'd note the mania and hysteria. Remind the client he was a father in his thirties, responsible and logical. Not a hitch-hiking Romeo with the ignorant and virile force of youth.

Yet Kozue ran my thoughts. Whatever suspicions I had about

who she was or what she did for a living were quashed by a storm of hormones clouding judgement. Beyond a classic beauty, her almost regal manner, and that gleaming, jet-black hair, was someone who zoomed in on my very self.

For three weeks I neither sent nor received a text. When I dared wonder what had happened my outcomes ranged from feeling like a stalker to imagining her murdered by the jealous boyfriend. Or gangster. Whoever he was, or whoever I imagined him to be, depending on my mood.

I rang her again. No answer. No idea what to do with myself, how to think. My office walls closing in.

It was a dazzling afternoon, and I skipped work and rode my bike along the bay, following the power lines that stretch fission from the nuclear plants in Chiba and Fukushima to the energy devouring metropolis.

The sea flickered and rippled, lapped against the wharf in a magnesium strobe. Couples strolled and old men fished, carefully baiting hooks and casting into the bright water. I cycled till dusk, hoping to ride out my infatuation. Eventually I stopped at a convenience store and bought a flavourless tuna sandwich. I sat on a bench outside a golf range and joylessly ate.

I took a picture of the bay with my phone, and sent it to Kozue.

Following my text into the sky, I imagined the scene bouncing off a satellite and appearing in her hand. Her screen would be silent. No sound of the planes that banked and climbed, the boats that motored and barely left a wake. Although I could hear the thwack of golf balls struck in the driving range, the after-swooshed whip of air and whistling flight, there was no thud on the green. Just an infinite climb. Satellites pinged in the dark of space, an orbit looped with dimpled spheres, my unanswered texts.

I put my phone on the bench and waited. I watched the screen until the sun went down and the pleasure boats glowed and cruised the harbour like luminous beetles.

十五

KOJI HAD A name. Her name. A wonderment when he typed her into a search engine and deleted the billions.

She posted pictures of the meals she ate. She wrote to her new friends, her mother in California. She posted pictures of herself, too. In his room she was ever-present. Hovered on a screen from his desktop.

Koji rented an apartment in a block due for demolition. Most of the other residents had moved out, and he was one of the last occupants on the floor. Ride the empty lift. Wander the halls. Returning each night to the sodium lobby where he met his reflection in the black glass. Another self leaving as he entered.

In the evenings he wiped and mopped his tiny kitchen. Cupboards full of bleach and spray. He talked to his grandmother when he cleaned, telling her about his day, complimenting her on food he ate as a child. He scrubbed and scoured because she was watching, expecting. He was a good boy when he did his chores. When he beat the futons and swept the tatami.

No matter how hard Koji cleaned his apartment, the cockroaches skittered across the work surface. These were the hours he wished he was ash. Sitting in the dark while the beetles ran.

Then she'd post something on-line, a comment or photo. A plan. And save him from himself.

十六

MAZZY HAD BEEN hassling me for a game of tennis since her arrival, and after her first week at school I took her up to the university to show her my office and play on the student courts.

"So this is where you experiment on people?"

"Conduct research."

"Experiment."

"Documenting the existence of national behaviour types in group performance under duress."

"Frankenstein."

More often than not I was losing these little exchanges. However, each time she got the better of me I felt a little prouder.

"This is just the halls, right?"

She was looking through the gates of the less than impressive back entrance to the campus. Walking distance from the glitz, noise and mania of Shibuya, the aged buildings hardly reflect the highest level of academia and education in the nation. Perhaps Mazzy was expecting the architectural grandeur of Cambridge or Oxford, or at least a Disneyesque attempt at history like Harvard or Princeton. Instead she got a shabby campus with a dirt baseball pitch and run-down buildings, as if giant cardboard boxes had been haphazardly dropped from the sky.

"I have one of the new offices," I began, watching her eyes rove across the dilapidated science labs. "They have another site, and whatever the state of the classrooms, the teaching is the best in the country."

"Sure, dad."

"I can see Fuji from my window on a clear day."

It was a moment I knew would be communicated to her mother, a sisterhood that I was forever excluded, the dork trying to befriend the It girls. Fashion, social media, sex, swimming and music, I was always the hanger-on.

"Where are the courts, dad?"

Except in tennis.

It was a sport we all excelled at, but here, and for once, I had the alpha male role confirmed. Although I do wonder if I'd played Lydia when we were both twenty one, without my eight year advantage of youth, whether she'd have got the better of me. Last time I stepped onto a court with Mazzy she'd run me close, a 6-4 set that she could've taken if she'd held her serve.

"Astroturf isn't your surface."

"What? Your days are numbered, dad. Gonna pound you into the court."

"No chance."

"Okay, if I win I get to go to the Kasabian concert in Yokohama."

"Doesn't matter, you're not going."

"Let's bet, then."

"Hold your horses."

I first wanted her to see my office and the lab. She made the loser L sign with her thumb and index finger, and we both laughed when I grabbed her hand and pressed it on her own forehead.

"Bully."

We wrestled, like how we used to when she was a little girl, before we broke away, embarrassed, remembering that she was now a young woman and I was the visiting professor at an esteemed university.

I signed her in at the reception and we went through to the lab, a basement hall fitted out to challenge and test various international groups working together. Early numbers backed up my hypothesis that the Japanese would out-perform other nations when group consensus must form rapidly and sub-consciously.

"There are cameras, there, there, and there."

I pointed to the corners of the room, the lenses set in pods like plastic swallow nests.

"Creepy."

"You've not lived in London enough. More cameras than people."
"That's fucked."
"Mazzy."
"You know that's the right word."
"Well."

I explained how we'd assembled teams of Japanese, Russians, Chinese, Turkish and Spanish, and set them time pressure tasks with completion rewards, and then recorded our observations of group adaptability and co-operation.

"I'm hoping to use the research in a paper on Japanese community structures and social harmony."

"Hmm."

She was either sceptical or bored. I took her up to my office on the top floor, a white walled corridor shared with visiting academics from around the world. When we got to my office she snooped around like a cat might sniff an unfamiliar room, before picking up the picture of the two of us at Yosemite.

"Haven't you got a more recent photo?"
"It's a great picture."
"I do look cute."
"You remember the trip?"
"Didn't we see a wolf?"
"A coyote."

She put down the picture and asked where Fuji was. I pointed at haze over the western ranges, and she hooded her eyes and scanned in disappointment.

"Come up again on a clear day."
"School's gonna be hectic." She looked again at the Yosemite photo. "Let's play tennis, dad."

We went down to the courts and I stretched and did a few jumping jacks to get the blood flowing. Mazzy was serving into the mesh fencing, reaching and snapping at the lobbed balls. She looked to have gained extra power from somewhere.

When she turned, and saw me flapping out another jumping jack, she laughed.

"Is that a dance?"

"A victory dance."

"For what? Making it onto the court."

The goading worked. "Right. Are you ready?" I was wound up and we hadn't even hit a ball.

Mazzy won the coin toss and let me serve, forgetting that no matter how much slower I was around the court than her, I could still put an ace past her flailing racquet.

"That's what the jumping jacks were for," I said, watching the ball whack into the fence as I took the first game.

"I have to get you cocky so you don't concentrate."

"Let's see this new serve."

She drummed the ball from the court to her palm, pressed it against the strings then stretched and lobbed, before hitting a curving serve that veered beyond my swishing racquet.

"Oh, oh. Dad."

"'Oh, oh,' what? I'm glad my money on your lessons is paying off."

I knew what to expect with her next serve, but the bounce and leap, combined with the banana swing and length, meant that I parried a floating return she dismissed with a clinical smash.

"It's gonna be a quick game."

"Don't count your chickens."

She took the game. And the next, breaking my serve with a whipped forehand that kicked off the astroturf. For a year she'd been quicker around the court, but now she was smarter too, and knew how to get me running. I spent the next two games sliding around like a drunken skater before it came down to set point.

"You want a time out?"

I was breathing like a geriatric, and the gristle of cartilage in my knee was clicking with each step.

"I'll take the time out when I take the set."

"Whatever."

I had one surge of adrenaline left for a big serve, and put an ace in the corner.

"Now the comeback."

"Of the century if you win this."

"You choked last time."

"No I didn't."

I was tempted to wind her up, start a nagging doubt. This was my chance to needle her into mistakes. My competitive streak in conflict with paternal encouragement.

"I'm not going to let you win, you know."

Her racquet-twirling crouch, poised, on her toes.

"Just to be kind."

"Serve," she shouted, before I heard an exasperated, "Fuck," under her breath.

Whatever the result, more damage would be done by handing her the victory. I took a breath and lobbed the ball. Beyond the arc of flight from hand to racquet, I sensed a figure watching from a bench beside the court, and I hit the serve late. The ball sat up for Mazzy to lash down the line, beyond my clumsy dive.

"Game, set, match. Ms Mazzy Sanderson."

Mazzy hurdled the net.

"I was put off."

"Erm, by what?" Mazzy looked around the empty courts.

"That guy was watching us. Well, you."

"What guy?"

I pointed towards the bench.

"Who?"

The seat was empty.

"Excuses. Face it. I beat you, fair and square."

"I swear there was someone there."

With a camera. Or perhaps just a phone.

"Don't be such a bad loser."

I must have imagined the watcher, hallucinated a disclaimer

to the point which had ended my reign as family tennis champion.

"I'm a good father. I let you win to encourage you."

"*Please.*"

I put my arm around her, admitted defeat.

"The student beats the sensei."

"Okay, okay," I agreed, and then pathetically claimed back some kudos by saying that victory was mine too, as it was a triumph for my DNA.

"Dad, that is so desperate. You were whupped."

She was right. I picked up my tracksuit top and limped off the court, while she positively skipped ahead.

十七

KOJI FIRST MET his new family on the top floor of an apartment block in Nishi-Azabu. It seemed like any other singles party for young professionals. A mix of guests standing around with drinks and chatting. Koji couldn't see the old woman in the room, and he nearly walked straight back out of the door, but a girl with a red birthmark spilling across her left cheek put a glass of apple juice into his hand.

"I'm Etsuko."

Koji introduced himself. Stuttering, he commented on the swanky apartment, the views of Roppongi Hills and Aomori Cemetery.

"You haven't been to a meeting before, have you?"

Koji said he didn't know why he was there.

"Wait till later," said Etsuko, sipping at her juice. "Chiho will explain."

For twenty minutes Koji hovered around the buffet, looked from the windows and avoided conversation. Then Chiho walked into the room wearing a white kimono. The guests wowed at her lambent appearance, and even Koji found himself politely applauding too.

There was a tatami mat in the front window facing the cemetery, and Chiho took her place on a large cushion next to three candles burning on the coffee table. Etsuko motioned Koji to sit with the group, and when the lights were turned down Chiho glowed like an effigy.

She sat with her eyes closed for a long time. Koji wanted to leave, but his way to the door was blocked by rows of folded legs. Partly, he wanted to go because he recognised something of his grandmother in this curious old woman. The way she perched herself on a cushion above the audience. The shock of white hair.

Yet here he was.

Nowhere else to go.

He stared at her, as did the others in the room. He waited, perhaps an hour. When he finally decided to stand up and walk out, she opened her eyes. Those piercing black stones. Her body motionless, as if only her pupils were living.

Koji was fixed in her gaze. He sat down, afraid. Chiho took a loud, exaggerated breath, and then let out a long, mournful hum. A sustained note of grief. Koji felt the reverberations in his sternum as she repeated the sound over and over, shuddering the room like a seismic tremor, as if her body had to expel the force before she was shaken apart.

Very clearly, Koji saw his grandmother at the kitchen stove, lifting udon from the pot, wreathed in steam.

Then a gasp from the audience, people shifting to see out of the window.

"Look, look," shrilled Etsuko, pointing beyond Koji's shoulder. "In the cemetery."

Koji knelt to get a better view.

"A light."

Yes. There was a light. Koji could see it too. A white ball rising above the treetops, lifting into the dark.

Chiho didn't turn to watch. She sang again, a thrumming note that fixed the family, her children. As if the line of song were an umbilical cord.

There would be speeches and prophecies. Rituals and pledges. Punishment for the transgressors. Orders to which Koji would feel no guilt in executing. Commands from the group, for the group. Not an individual.

十八

I FORGOT WHO I was, sitting in the air-conditioned taxi, new clothes and shoes that pinched. The white-gloved driver was silent, never registering my presence. More computer graphic than any actual life, my character was driven through the Tokyo circuitry as if I were just code in the city's teeming programme.

It was the night after Kozue had replied to my picture of the bay, a buzzed text instructing me to meet her at a Shinjuku hotel.

I got out of the cab and nodded to the bowing doorman, before sitting awkwardly on a leather cube chair in the reception. It was a five star hotel, orchids and a fountain. Legions of staff in pressed uniforms. I was preparing to tell Kozue that she was cold, leaving me to worry about where she'd vanished. I was ready to be angry and curt, dismiss her advances.

Until she walked across the polished floor of the lobby, tall and commanding in a tight black skirt and shimmering blouse. Stunning. Her clicking heels forcing heads to turn and stare.

I kissed her on the cheek, lightly.

"You've lost weight," she said.

"I've been running a lot."

"In this heat?"

"Along the river at night, when the air has cooled."

"We should eat, early."

A doorman flagged down another taxi and we slid onto the back-seat. In very formal Japanese she instructed the driver where to go.

Then she grabbed my hand and locked her fingers through mine, gripping. I was never short of things to say on a date, not that I'd even use this word to describe the encounter, but I didn't want to spoil the sensation with clumsy jokes.

"You knew I was going to come and see you, didn't you?"

I couldn't find the restaurant again if my life depended on it. Perhaps it doesn't exist now. It's possible that it never did, considering the way things have worked out.

From what I recall, the taxi stopped beneath one of a thousand concrete sections of Tokyo's elevated highways. Not a door or paper lantern in sight. I looked around, saw empty lots and abandoned office blocks.

Kozue took ten thousand yen from her wallet and gave it to the white-gloved driver. He took the note and scanned the shadows, nervous, confused at the final destination of an elegantly dressed couple in a deserted back street.

We stepped out of the car. Once the taxi had turned the corner, it was very quiet. Just the occasional swish of traffic on the highway above.

"You have the right place?"

"You don't trust me?"

The question was beyond her ability to find a restaurant. And perhaps I didn't trust her. Still, I followed her into the lobby of a brand new apartment building and waited by the lift. The doors slid open and we stepped inside. Kozue pressed the button to take us down to the basement. When the doors closed I leant over and kissed her on the lips, inhaled a scent that jangled my bones. When the doors opened again the lights went out, leaving us in total darkness.

Kozue took my hand, and we followed a tiny red point beamed onto the floor. Once my eyes adjusted I made out a figure carrying a small torch, sliding back a paper screen to reveal a large room filled with what looked like giant, luminous chrysalids. Pods of light dotting the darkness, murmurs of hushed conversations, glasses softly clinked together. The shadow led us towards a glow and parted the curtain. Two cushions and a low black table set with copper chopsticks and a large white candle.

Kozue told me to take off my shoes, and I did, a boy in her company. Sitting on the floor with my legs crossed, in a restaurant where a phantom maître d' walked a void in utter silence. I jumped when a menu was passed through the diaphanous silk by a veiled waiter.

"We won't see anyone else," said Kozue. "They won't let us leave at the same time as another couple."

I read the menu. Salmon and lobster, cuts of tuna. Kozue asked if she could choose, and I gladly let her order through the curtain to a voice in the dark.

While she spoke I watched her wide mouth, the sheen of lip gloss. And the delicate swish of her eyebrows, drawn on, of course, but all the more perfect because the arcs were her creation.

After she passed the menu back she said, "You're going to ask me what I've been doing, why I didn't call."

I was. But the disdain in her tone for needing this information put a stop to the question.

"I'm thrilled you're here."

"And that's enough?"

"It's a lot."

The waiter appeared again, briefly, setting down a tray holding a bottle of sake and two tiny cups. Kozue poured, and I made a toast.

"To things we can't see."

We drank, the sharp rice wine a jolt. Kozue took my empty cup and poured another. She passed me the sake and asked if I was afraid of the dark.

"Just what's in it."

I told her about hitch-hiking Shikoku, the woodcutter and the tunnels, walking pitch black roads under mountains. I told her about the kimono salesman too, but not the pearls. How I should have given them to my wife on our wedding day.

"You know what a *tanuki* is?"

"A raccoon."

"And a *kitsune*?"

"Fox."

"Old stories say they can change into humans, take on our form when they want to trick us. People used to believe that a beautiful woman at night, walking alone, was most likely a transformed fox."

"Now I'm suspicious."

She laughed. "You can check." She leant before the candle and told me to look at her profile on the curtain. "A fox can be human, but they can't hide the shadow of their tail."

She was very close, stretching on all fours to get the right angle from the flame. I admired her shadow, the curve of her slim hips. Then I looked into her eyes, the brown iris and black pupil, merged.

"What do you see?"

Then another voice, the veiled waiter and a tray of food. The fish arrived, impaled on a stick in the middle of a plate. When Kozue took a piece of flesh from its back, the fin twitched.

"It moved."

"It's fresh," she said. "That's all."

I told her I'd eaten snake in China, crocodile in Australia, and that I'd try anything but cat.

"Good." She prized off a piece of fish, deftly picking out the bones with her chopsticks. "When the apes climbed down from the trees and started walking, the cats got together and called a meeting. They were about to evolve into a species beyond humans, but they decided to remain as cats and have us wait on them."

"That's it," I said. "You're a shape shifting cat."

十九

IT WAS AFTER Koji came back from Mount Fuji without the girl from Hokkaido that he was ejected from the group.

The old woman had given him life.

Meaning and belonging.

Then killed him.

He was stunned at the city without his family, without orders to act upon. For two days he walked the streets like a simpleton, sitting on steps and watching the traffic, horrified at the thought of being alone.

Then the rage.

He booked into a capsule hotel and stockpiled petrol for a week. The morning he transported fuel over to the Tokyo headquarters police had cordoned off the car park and raided the building. Officers in latex gloves carried out bags of clothes and bundles of white sheets. A glass tank filled with a colony of white ants.

Koji drove straight to the ruin of his grandmother's house in Kobe. Apart from the removal of her body, almost nothing had been touched. Her empty slippers in the porch. A tea cup on the kitchen table. And moss, growing up the curtains, on the seats of the chairs and the floor cushions. There were mice in her wardrobe, blinking and squirming when he switched on the light.

He spent the next week washing, cleaning, and killing. Poisoning rodents and insects. He found snake eggs in the garage, sparrows nesting in the loft. Her rotting kimonos. He slept in his car at night, or walked through the moonlit paddies.

Carefully, he peeled their damp and warped wedding photo from the frame, tore away the half containing his grandfather, and slipped his grandmother into his pocket. Then he took the cans of petrol from his car and poured throughout the rooms, soaking the rotten tatami and flooding the kitchen.

He was there when the firemen arrived. The wooden house incandescent, burning like a hole in the dark. Beams crumbling like blackened matchsticks, the melting glass. Above the sparks and shooting flames, in the luminous folds of smoke, he saw his grandmother. Young and pale, the virgin bride, rising from the ash with a gown of stars.

二十

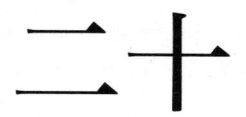

THE SUNDAY AFTER our tennis match I took Mazzy to Hibiya park and sat in the manicured square, a favourite sun-trap bordered with rosebushes. Towers of finance soared above the surrounding maple trees, whose crimson, star-shaped leaves, would fall to our feet and be studied.

We ate croissants and drank coffee, watching gangs of crows shoo stray cats off the benches and prepare a seat for their meal rifled from the bins. The crows stood on the metal rim and yanked out cans and bento boxes, throwing down remains to the birds waiting on the path, hopping and skipping with excitement. Rather than fighting and bickering like scavengers, they worked together. For any packaging that proved difficult to open, a crow would stand on the lid as the others tugged and ripped the plastic apart. One lively pair seemed to be playing a game with a newspaper, taking it in turns to jump on the pages while the other crow pulled along their passenger. Then abruptly they got bored and tore the stories into shreds, feathering the lawn with a failing Euro and bankrupt states, the bullet-ridden body of a lynched dictator. Occasionally they glanced around to see who might be watching, eyes blinking like a gun scope.

"Crows are going to take over the world," said Mazzy, pulling out her sketch book.

I told her about an experiment at Oxford University, the crow that bent a length of wire and hooked food from the end of a boiling tube.

"Lots of animals use stuff. Monkeys crack nuts with rocks."

"They don't adapt the rock. The crow visualised the tool, and then created it."

"I want a pet crow."

Mazzy was shading a beak, circling an eye, leaving a sliver of page bare for the glint of light that always finds the crow pupil. One bird hopped away from the smorgasbord of trash littering the gardens. It stared at us sat on the bench, cocked its head.

"What are you thinking, handsome?"

She sketched, the scratch of pencil in the windless quiet. That and the cawing crows, the birds in the treetops calling to the birds in the park.

"Do you want to see a film later?"

She turned the pad, put her finger to a pencil line and smudged out a feather.

"That's a nice touch."

With both hands she held the picture before her.

"You have an audience."

Crows on the branches seemed to be passing judgement on her rendering too, and Mazzy held her pad towards the tree. They shifted on their perch and cawed.

"Glad you like it."

"Film later?"

"I'm meeting Larissa in Omotesando."

"Larissa?"

"From school."

"You didn't tell me."

"You didn't ask."

I shrugged. Tried to hide a feeling of being slighted.

"She's cool. Her mom's Japanese and her dad's from Brooklyn."

"What are you going to do?"

"Hang out. Stuff."

I walked with her to Ginza station. I felt like the dawdling geek making the most of his time with a cooler kid. Only here a fortnight and she already had her own life.

"Call if you get lost."

"I can already ask for directions. *Hibiya koen wa doko desu ka?*"

"Your pronunciation's better than mine."

Her phone buzzed and she looked at the screen. "Later, dad." Then she jogged down the station steps and left me wondering which direction to walk.

I backtracked and took a stroll around the Imperial Palace. Usually the open space was a relief from claustrophobic Tokyo, but today it felt cold and empty so I went back into Ginza and hovered around the department stores. After a weak cappuccino in a smoky café I headed towards a curry shop beneath an archway of the Yamanote line. A jazz soundtrack accompanied by the rumble of passing trains scored the restaurant scene of single men tucking into cheap food. I ate and thought of nothing, just the sauce on the spoon, occasionally looking up to watch shadows pass by on the opaque window.

Then I zipped up my coat and walked outside.

She was stopped by a bank. A woman in a kimono, checking her hair and smoothing her silk in the mirrored glass. She wore the print of a flying crane, a feathery scarf. Rouged cheeks and a delicate, pale neck. I stared at her reflection while she rummaged in her handbag. After she found the lipstick, she looked up and saw me. Against the white of her powdered face, her eyes were nearly black. For one jolting second I thought it was her, before she shuffled away, carefully lifting up her precious hem.

**

The sky was electric, bright after the dark restaurant. A blaze of bulbs and headlights, the beacon of Tokyo Tower.

Again, there was no one on the street until the taxi rounded the corner. Kozue instructed the driver to take us back to the hotel, and then took my hand and pressed it between her palms. I asked her how long she was staying, but she ignored my question and lightly ran her nails along the inside of my forearm.

An express lift whisked us from the lobby. The corner room jutted over the twinkling city. Warning lights on taller buildings, helicopters buzzing like fireflies. Kozue switched off the lamp and left the curtains open. When we stripped our skin was the flicker of neon, pale bodies in the acetylene tremor.

There was a fatalistic vigour to sex. A fear that we could disintegrate if we let ourselves subside, that the world was not enough beyond our desperation. She pulled my hair and bit my chest, warned me not to come until she clamped her legs around the small of my back and bound her orgasm into mine.

Flopped together and faint, we slept. I woke up to find her standing at the window. Naked and glowing, as if a projection of the city. I said her name and she shut the curtains and came back to bed, laying on her back and closing her eyes. Her hair spread upon the pillow like a black star.

The questions I wanted to ask seemed infantile, words that would ruin the aesthetic. The fantasy I'd conjured would be destroyed by the fact. So I slept again, merged the unchecked truth with dream.

She woke me at dawn by kissing my stomach. Tickled by her long, silky hair. I ran my palm along her jawline, and she took my thumb deep into her mouth, curling her tongue around my knuckles before grabbing my wrist and pulling my hand away.

"Do something for me."

She wanted me to kneel on the floor.

"Like you did in my apartment."

I knelt on the floor and pulled her hips against my mouth, circling her wetness before pushing inside. Kissing, kissing. She dug her nails in the base of my skull when she came, hard, forcing her pelvis against my face. Her thighs trembled and tightened before she broke away and collapsed onto the carpet. After she caught her breath we climbed onto the bed and she straddled me, slowly, clutching my wrists and holding them above my head. She leant down and kissed me, bit my lip. Then she gyrated her hips, a quickening rhythm. I arched from the sheets, a muscle-taut shudder when we came again, locked together.

We lay like twins in a womb, lit by the pulse of Tokyo pressing through the curtain. She brushed her lips along my shoulder, my chest. I felt weightless. Either that or dead. Gloriously dead, because this woman could bring me back to life. She already had.

"In my apartment," she said. "When you knelt on the floor. That was first time I'd come."

"Ever?"

"Well, with a man."

Perhaps she was lying. Pandering to my fragile masculinity.

"You like women?"

She shrugged. "A month ago I went to see a therapist. A sex therapist. I thought there might be something biologically wrong. Some medical reason I'd never had an orgasm."

I had both male and female friends who specialised in sex therapy. All wanting a career in a strand of behaviour, they had their own quirks and foibles, and I was therefore sceptical of any professional in the field.

"She was in her forties, silver in her hair. There was a family picture on her desk, two boys and her husband on a beach. She was serious, but not cold. She told me that it was nothing that couldn't be fixed, and that although our minds are weaker than our bodies, thoughts can be changed, released."

Kozue shifted onto her elbow so she could see my face, that I was listening.

"Then she said I was very beautiful. That I had something that men would always want to take away, or destroy, and that because I already knew this I'd never let my barrier down, my defences."

"You did to me."

"In the bar. You looked at me like the rest of the world didn't exist."

"It didn't."

That sheen of hair, her lucent skin. She was right. Outside the room there was nothing.

"You were almost glowing, a phantom."

"No." Kozue shook her head. "I'm real."

She pinched my arm.

"Ouch."

"See."

She rolled onto her back and stared at the ceiling. "The therapist said she needed to check there wasn't a physiological problem, and that I had to take my clothes off and lay on the bed. I did as she asked. The therapist went into her cupboard and put on a latex glove. She asked questions about any discomfort or pain during sex. I told her there was just a coldness, and she apologised and said she had to look more closely."

Then Kozue told me about her orgasm. How the therapist slipped her hands across her labia, talking, insisting that she was the director of her own body, the one who decided whether the man deserved her.

"And I came, right on her hand. I grabbed her wrist and held her fingers inside me."

**

Two women fighting is the kanji for jealousy, *shitto*. One woman has an arrow, the other a rock. The kanji for tree is a picture of a tree. A forest is three trees. Although the strokes and marks of the writing system came easily to my studious mind, my conversational Japanese was too formal to ring up a hostess club in Hiroshima and ask after a woman who'd worked there five years ago. And it hardly seemed the appropriate favour to be asking Yamada.

Still, I wanted to know where she was. I had to know. The woman on the street in Ginza jarred my being. For that brief second I thought it was Kozue, it was as if a train had rattled down the track of my spine.

One man who could help me was a guy from Chicago named Lenny Brick. He owned an attic bar on a Roppongi backstreet, and though I hadn't been in since my return, I'd walked past to see if he'd survived the post-earthquake exodus when *gaijin* had abandoned the country like rats from a sinking ship. The restaurants, clubs and import shops that relied on the homesick foreigner had sunk with the economy. However, The Shotgun, his ramshackle blues bar, was still afloat.

Lenny was a morning man, meaning he'd still be awake when the sun came up. Frazzled by a night serving drinks and smoking Marlboro Red. To get him in a good mood, and sober, I needed to pay him a visit during working hours. And that meant after midnight.

The evening I decided to drop by The Shotgun I sat in the living room waiting for Mazzy to go to bed. Now she was in the swing of school and study, she came home, ate, tweeted and Skyped her mother, before crashing out to wake at seven and do it all over again the next day.

Flicking through TV channels, skimming past inane panel shows and cardboard newscasters, I had one eye on her bedroom and one eye on the screen. When I was sure she was asleep I pushed her door ajar. She was curled around her journal, iPhone on the pillow.

I put my shoes on and slipped out.

I felt guilty sneaking out of the apartment, but not irresponsible. After all, Mazzy was nearly sixteen, and would scoff at my mollycoddling if she knew I was worried about leaving her alone for a couple of hours.

There is a particular smell in Roppongi. An odour of stale nights accumulated in the alleys and the drains. Beer seeps through bodies and into the sewers, embedding the memory of an evening into brickwork and concrete, a record of events where the neurones have failed, deleted through shame or chemical abuse. Even on a sunlit afternoon, walking between one of the gleaming new shopping cathedrals, you might catch the whiff of an illicit encounter in a shadowed doorway, see a hunch-backed crone mopping the steps of a bar, rinsing ashtrays or drying beer towels. There is the feeling of seeing a stage stripped and bare.

Then the sun sets and the lights shine, and the meretricious glamour returns and deceives. In the painted face of an average girl is a beautiful woman, and the gaudily dressed gangster is stylish and charming. Alcohol is the potion, the spell to fairyland.

The last time I frequented The Shotgun I was a borderline drunk. An American AA manifesto would have me down as a chronic case, but an English group would laugh and say I was basically teetotal. Still, I'd outgrown the barfly, and had no desire to sit in a dingy room and trade stories that would be lost in a fog of tobacco and alcohol. I wonder if the history students of the future will find our belief in God more baffling than smoking in public places.

Besides, the only part of Japan I ever feel unsafe is Roppongi. Not because of the Japanese, but my fellow foreigners. Occasionally the yakuza will stage a showdown with a hapless traffic cop brave enough, or foolish enough, to enforce a parking ticket on a tinted window. The geeky boy in a blue uniform, face to face with a tanned and buff gangster. Yet the unflinching policeman will absorb any bellowed threats, before a slow, processional drive to another prohibited space for the next performance of muscle flexing.

When I first ventured onto these seedy streets, the twenty-something in search of adventure and experience, sex, the harrying pimps were Russian or Iranian, cutting profits with the local mobsters for the right to work their pavements. Now the dregs selling blowjobs and cocaine are mostly Nigerian and Ghanian, fighting each other for the remaining scraps of patrons, a customer base shrunk to the well-heeled banker or curious tourist. Gone are the naïve boys from US bases, teens from boondock towns old enough to join the Marines but too young to buy a beer in the country they pledged to die for. When the Twin Towers came down and Bush deployed the GIs to Iraq they were allowed off base for weekend blow-outs. After necking cans of Asahi and Kirin they'd hit the bars and the brothels and, if they were lucky, wake up in

Military Prisons, not the hands of the Japanese police. Or the local gangs. Here the MPs, or the cops, held little sway. The go-to man was Lenny, brokering deals between the mobs and the Army.

And now, hopefully, an agent for my own investigations.

When I swung open the door he had his back turned and was fiddling with the music volume, a Howlin' Wolf track. It was early, and there was only a young Japanese couple at the far end of the counter. He still had currency from all over the world pasted onto the walls, along with graffiti he encouraged to be carved into the wooden panelling: names and states, football teams and insults.

He spun around and saw me. "Motherfucker."

"My pleasure."

He cracked a wide smile and palm-slapped into a big handshake. "You finally come to put me in the nut house?"

He poured a beer and sloppily pushed it across the counter. We chinked glasses and drank. Skin sagged around his cheekbones. Scars from wives and wars had merged into wrinkles, but he still had his smile, the gold tooth flashing.

"I'm surprised you're still alive."

"It's a daily miracle."

Though very different animals, we ultimately shared the hunt for human truth. With Lenny it was a direct show of feelings, a blunt force of animus. My quest was to measure and define what makes us who we are, observe and record. He wore his sub-conscious on his sleeve, perhaps my alter ego, the machismo I was cautious of baring. While I read journals on the nature of aggression, or studied the evidence for attraction through DNA information communicated by scent, Lenny would just as happily fuck or fight.

"I know I've been here too long when you walk back in."

His wobbly hands and bloodshot eyes. The signature Hawaiian shirt, unusually for him, ironed and clean. Past the Ray Charles tattoo on his arm was a cluster of nicotine patches.

"Gimme some news."

I told him about my return to England, skimmed across the

years, the book and the research, and avoided talk about Mazzy. I didn't want her presence where I'd obliterated my senses and leered over women half my age. I came here after Kozue had waltzed into my life, and straight back out again. Solace in the piss and vinegar of forgotten bar talk. When I asked Lenny if he still saved soldiers from the yakuza, he shook his head.

"They hardly let the kids off base. Place is dying. You know what I saw last week? A fucking hobo playing a harmonica outside a shuttered restaurant. 'This is Tokyo motherfucker.' That's what I said to him."

"It is quiet."

"The quake killed my custom. They got scaredy cat over some radiation cloud and quit."

"And the Army doesn't need your services?"

"Well, I did have one punk to save a month ago. A new scam. This captain I know brought him over. Kid wakes up in a love hotel, no sign of the girl he took in there. Walks into the toilet and there's blood up the walls, on his hands, all over his face. His ID is missing, and all he has is a business card and a number. Finds out he's got accusations that need to be paid off, that he'd 'done things.' Comes in here, sits right where you are, begging me he did nothing wrong. He's like, 'I swear on my life the bitch drugged me.'"

Lenny had said nothing in response to the young rifleman. When the army came to him with a problem they needed fixing, he first let them speak. Watched for lies rather than listened. Carl Rogers with a bar stool replacing the couch, whisky instead of water.

"This kid's like, 'All that bullshit about the coke and the whores. What the fuck. Three beers and I'm unconscious. Never. I've been drinking since I was in High School and three beers never blacked me. Even when I was drinking Crazy Horse.'"

Intrigued by Lenny's self-proclaimed skills at reading physical cues, I'd once given him a facial recognition test, a series of photos to decipher which subject was faking a smile and which was genuine. He'd scored twenty out of twenty.

"The kid's already done a tour in Iraq. Tells me about his ass twitching in a helicopter dropping like a stone, that he was more scared walking into that bathroom."

Lenny had watched his hands. How the kid wiped his brow, the sweat marks on the cuffs of his grey hoodie, the Duke basketball logo, childish. A coat of arms no help to him here.

"Thing is, I ain't got the sway I used to have. But I'd heard a couple of stories about the extortion, and once I worked out where the girls were hanging out it didn't take long to speak to the men running the racket."

"Had he done anything?"

Lenny laughed. "The kid? Nothing apart from a shot of rohypnol. The blood was the kind of shit you get at a joke shop. Thing is, these finance guys who ain't got the balls the soldiers have wake up and empty their bank accounts. They got kids and wives. What, they're gonna go home and say, 'Honey I took a prostitute to a love hotel, got wasted, and woke up with blood all over the walls.'"

I changed the subject, asked him about his life, his health. "76 days dry." He pointed to a calendar on the wall, the dates crossed out with a marker pen. "And I'm running a fucking bar. I should get a medal."

"A new liver."

"I can get you a Filipino one if you ever need it."

He smiled, and I presumed he was joking. Then again he was the kind of guy that could arrange a black market organ deal.

"How's your Japanese coming along?"

"I can read about ten kanji. And most of those are to do with food. My grammar is fucked up all over the place. But I can sit and drink sake with a yakuza boss, tell him jokes till he pisses his pants."

Lenny talked about his divorce, his new wife, and that I was too old to be single. I reminded him I had a daughter and was about to ask the Kozue favour when a muscle-bound Serbian came in with a Japanese girl. Lenny shook his hand and punched his shoulder. The motherfucker welcome. I shuffled along the counter and drank my beer while Lenny laughed and joked with the couple.

Then a strange pause. As if a flaw in relativity. When I caught my face in the mirror behind the bar, only halfway down my pint and already feeling light headed, I was practically time travelling. Connecting the past and the present. The feeling, a recollection, that sitting here five years ago I'd looked into the mirror and seen myself at this very moment.

I drained my glass, told Lenny I was heading out.

"Already?"

"It's a school night."

I'd hate for Mazzy to wake and find me gone. I put on my jacket and opened the door.

"Come see me at the weekend," Lenny called. "You came in here for something, I know you did."

**

Mazzy carried home books and files, piled them on the living room table, and bought a pair of speakers for her laptop. Like a liberating army parachuting in from the sky, she spread her territory from her bedroom to the rest of apartment in rapid drops of possessions.

She freed me from a locked self. A personality ruled by the despot of work and singledom. I felt younger, connected. Not only with my daughter, but the groups I was measuring. What had been nodes in a circuit board were again sentient beings, people. Though my freedom came with certain conditions. I was still the president of my own country, my apartment, but the occupying forces dictated when and where I was allowed this expression.

After a day analysing reams of data, trying to dislodge the night with Lenny from my thoughts, I came back to thumping music and two of Mazzy's new friends flopped across the sofa, a box of ravaged doughnuts on the counter.

First I was introduced to Legolas, a tall and gangly Swedish boy, who was polite enough to put down his hood and shake my hand.

And then her latest 'best friend,' Larissa, a sassy girl with a row of multi-coloured braces across teeth that already looked perfect.

"My mom bought your book."

"Tell her thank you."

"She doesn't agree with a lot of it, though."

"Oh, well."

"But she read it."

Mazzy asked what I was doing, which translated to, *Get out dad, we were having fun till you turned up.*

"You can have the living room," I told her. "I've things to be getting on with."

"Do you a have a Swedish sample group?" asked the elongated boy. "Like, we're so similar. I mean. Robots."

"Tell him about *largum*," said Larissa, Mazzy sighing because it meant I'd gatecrash a minute or two longer.

"If you go to someone's house for coffee in Sweden, and they ask how much sugar do you want, everyone just says, '*Largum*.' The usual. But like, what's the usual? Everything is *largum*. How many potatoes. *Largum*. How much gravy?"

"*Largum*," said Larissa.

"*Largum*," he shrugged.

I finally got a word in, explained that countries with large middle classes showed a strict obedience to the norm, like Japan, and that the most effective groups demonstrated a subconscious consensus. I was about to expand when Mazzy told Legolas he could just read my book. I grabbed a copy off the shelf and handed it over. He looked at the cover, said, "Cool," and then fanned the pages as if he were hoping to find a flip cartoon in one of the corners before putting it down on the sofa and asking me if it was on Kindle.

"Let's get some maccha ice cream," suggested Larissa.

The team agreed. Within minutes they had shipped out, a cursory, "Later, dad," from Mazzy as she pulled the door shut.

I walked over to the box of doughnuts, took a half-eaten French vanilla and ate it while looking out of the window at the apartment block opposite, every balcony empty, blinds drawn.

I wrote the book because of Kozue. Not because I wanted to forget her, but to direct my energy into something else before I had a meltdown.

No. That's not entirely true, either. I wanted to understand what she'd told me the last time I saw her in Inokashira Park.

We'd sat on a bench in dying sunlight. Shrilling cicadas vibrated the air with a deafening song. Not that I could blame the insects for singing so loudly, only airborne for a few days after years beneath the soil.

I spoke to Kozue about my research, the cult lives I studied. The young, intelligent professionals who left careers and families to wear white and predict Doomsday. She listened, nodded, and said I should study the yakuza.

"Your life is the group. Everything you do is for others. The individual is swallowed by this huge creature, and whatever this creature does, this monster, you're part of it."

She played with the sleeve of her top, twisted it through her fingers. "I was the high school archery champion." She held out her arms, proud with an invisible bow. "On horseback."

I asked if she still practised, and she loosed an imaginary arrow at a crow swooping across the lake.

"I'm busy with other things."

I sat and watched her, waited. I felt I was a close to history, truth. For a month we'd been meeting in hotels and onsens, erasing thought with body. Sex, not biography.

She pushed her hair behind her ears, that pale neck. "I'm from a rich family. Well, was. Old money. A proud father." She paused, looked for the cicadas shrilling in the trees. "Ruined."

I thought she was going to tell me more. A story that I did and didn't want to hear. I imagined blackmail and extortion, the indentured daughter in the seedy club. But nothing. When the setting sun filtered through the leaves, she warned that the mosquitoes would start biting. "Let's go on the lake."

Legend has it that Inokashira lake is cursed, and that lovers who dare to row its surface are doomed.

Neither of us were superstitious. And perhaps only one of us was a lover.

We drifted in the final streaks of daylight. The bump of the oarlocks. The golden droplets pearling on the blade. Kozue trailed her fingers, and then took off her shoes and dipped her feet. I studied her features. In the lengthening shadows was the foreboding that I'd never see them again. Her noble, yet feminine nose. Those high, feline cheekbones. Her laser stare offset by the warmth of her sumptuous mouth. Then her white toes, luminescent in the dark water.

Remnants of the day flared through the trees, and the lake blazed. We were floating on the corona of the sun. When a tower block hid the gloaming I rowed into the one remaining sunbeam, before that too was swallowed by the shade.

We lay down in the boat and kissed. What joy to feel like a traveller in my own life, with perhaps even the promise of hers. I looked at the first stars, bright in a patch of unfettered sky. There was no barrier between us and the rest of the universe, as if we could row along the Milky Way and watch the galaxies eddy in our wake.

Then reality arrived, sudden and unwelcome. Chimes sounded that the park was closing, and we paddled back to the moorings.

I told her not to go.

I told her she could tell me anything.

But the shore broke the spell. An odd, disturbing moment. After tying up the boat we were walking around the lake when a crow swooped from the dark and picked a sparkly grip from Kozue's hair.

"Did it scratch you?"

She watched the crow fly into the trees, the flash of silver in a talon. "Is that a good omen," she wondered. "Or a bad one?"

**

Rumour has it that Tokyo is too small for its population, and that if everyone came out of their apartments at the same time, the city would burst. Jammed onto a rush hour train, or marching along the morning pavement with the ranks of commuters, one may feel this is true. Yet the crowds have a measured step. Give me the record breaking footfall passing through Shinjuku station rather than the mania of Oxford Circus on a Saturday afternoon.

A contentious chapter in *Gangs, Groups and Belonging* pontificates on the survival of the obedient gene, where I argue that those who transgress in a society propelled by adherence to strict social and moral codes would be marginalised, and therefore less likely to pass on a rebellious trait.

Yamada was a key proponent of this theory, as it supported his negative angle on the unthinking masses, and how Japan was shrinking into economic and cultural oblivion. Without defeat in 1945, he argued, and the financial and military advantages of the Marshal plan keeping their historically wronged neighbours at bay, Japan would be fodder for China and Russia. He'd nearly been chased out of the faculty following a TV appearance. Unfairly edited, as he'd concluded his attack on blind conformity was driven by his patriotism, his sound bite riled the political right into action. Two days later he found an empty petrol can on his car seat, a red, rising sun, crudely painted over the label.

When we met for a bowl of ramen at lunch, he asked how my welcome lecture was coming along. "Not too many jokes, I hope."

I nearly spat out my soup. I'd clean forgotten about the presentation.

"I bet you're going to tell the Japanese audience how great they are."

I pinched a gyoza parcel between my chopsticks and dipped it in chilli oil. "I'm going to talk about building a dam."

"A metaphor."

"No. Dam building."

I crunched garlic and mince and chewed slowly, stoking my train of thought.

"The existence of a group soul," I said, rather dramatically, name dropping South African naturalist Eugene Marais and his colony of white ants, the evidence for a communal psyche, as well as the pioneering research on cricket teams by Doctor Jain Burdett, before I began the anecdote about Japanese schoolchildren building a dam on a summer camp I worked as an English teacher.

"Without any instructions, the kids leapt off the bus and ran to play in the stream that cut through the picnic area. The braver, more daring boys and girls splashed into the water, while the rest of the group began collecting rocks. Big, small, flat and pointed. Some rocks needed two people to carry them down the bank, others were passed along a chain of hands. Each and every child was an integral part of the construction. Within ten minutes of harmonious labour, the stream had been turned into a pool. This metre high feat of impromptu engineering, completed without any arguments or accidents, filled me with joy."

Yamada lifted the last of his noodles to his mouth. Then he picked up the bowl and drank the remaining soup.

"That's just the introduction," I added. "Then I'll talk social evolution, Bill Hamilton, what he might have theorised if he'd sat and recorded people in Tokyo station, not Waterloo."

Yamada was quiet, teasing any nonsense out of me. He put his bowl down. "Japan is the glass half full, *ne?*"

I copied his ramen drinking technique by picking up the bowl and tipping pork soup into my stomach.

"And Britain is half empty?"

Perhaps he was right. Simple, clear wisdom, as usual.

However, he didn't know that one variable to my shining optimism was the possibility of seeing Kozue again. I hadn't heard from her since that night in Inokashira Park, since I'd flown back to England and failed to pass off my infatuation as a holiday romance.

The giddy thought that I could speak with her once more, that I could make the ghost of this beautiful woman seemingly reappear, had me entranced.

**

The Shotgun was busy, bouncing with a crackly bluegrass number that had drinkers tapping feet and raising voices. Lenny had another guy serving, and once I bought a beer he came over with a drink and sat with me at a window table.

"Is that iced tea?"

"Tannin is good for you."

I sipped my Asahi, resisting the urge to down the glass.

"Pitch it, man. What you looking me up for? You're too old and wise to be fucking about in dive bars?"

"Easy on the old part."

"Shit," he laughed. "I'd lived a hundred lives by the time I was thirty, and I'm forty fucking five next year."

We chinked glasses to our forties, and I asked if he remembered Kozue.

"I remember you talking about her like she was some princess. You got no photos?"

"I wouldn't show you if I had."

"You know what. I think you constructed this dream woman in your lab. Like that 80s film, Weird Science, where they get Kelly LeBrock to appear in her bra and panties."

I shook my head. Told him that Kozue had vanished, and how I'd tried to get in touch with her again but had no luck.

"You're still pining for her?"

"Not exactly pining."

Lenny slurped tea through a bendy straw, like a kid finishing a milkshake. "Never good to hunt old flames. People change. Maybe you had some obsession."

"I did."

"And if you see her again now, wrinkles, grey hair."

"No, no. She'll age gracefully."

"I'm talking about you, motherfucker."

I took another gulp of beer. Then I explained that she'd worked at a club in Hiroshima, and wondered if he could ring them up and get some information.

"A hostess club giving out numbers of their girls?" He shook his head. "I have to think about the angle on this."

He took an ice cube from his glass and crunched it loudly. Then he nodded. "I got it. Follow me."

We went up the narrow staircase to a little office he kept above the bar. On the wall behind his desk were pictures of him with his kids, two daughters on his shoulders, the absent wife. Framed over the door was a shot of him in a baseball uniform holding aloft a golden, oversized trophy.

"You should hang that in the bar."

"And remind myself what a fucking mess I've degenerated into. That's what I'm trying to tell you."

He picked up the phone and sat down. He got the club number from the operator and then pre-dialled a number that would block his own. "I don't want some gangster turning up here because you've been dicking around with his woman."

"It's not like that."

"You don't know shit."

I sat on the corner of the desk, watched and listened. His whole body transformed when he spoke Japanese. Most of the fluent speaking foreigners I know have this power to mirror the body language needed to empower the syntax. They can bend and bow at the right moment, act out the deferential employee or thankful guest. Lenny became the swaggering, senior male, dropping his voice to a croaky bass. I heard him say Kozue a couple of times, and when he got no joy he snapped as if chastising an underling, before nodding to me and putting the phone down without so much as a thank you to the person he'd spoken with.

"I want a fucking Oscar or something."

"They told you."

"If I was still smoking I'd light a cigar. I made out I owned a club here, dropped a couple of names, and bam."

"And?"

"He thinks she might have left, but she was here."

"Tokyo?"

He nodded. "Last he knew she was working for The Island." Lenny rubbed his thumb across his fingers. "Hope you got some yen to walk in there with."

That train was rattling along my spine.

Lenny whipped out a drawer from his desk. "Fuck I could light one up." He rummaged around and found a pack of chewing gum and stuffed two strips into his mouth.

"You be careful somewhere like that."

"It's just a hostess bar, right?"

"They're money traps run by gangsters."

"Is this one dodgy?"

"Come on, man. They all are. The girls sit around pouring drinks and clapping when some old fart sings out of tune. It's a merry dance to get the guy in bed and for the girl to get paid without feeling like a whore."

I waffled something about geishas and tradition, and Lenny laughed. "Call it what you want. Oldest profession in the world."

"I'll sit in the club and have a drink. What could be simpler?"

Lenny blew a pink bubble with his gum, and then burst it like a firecracker. "You need to put down fifty grand just to get a conversation."

I shrugged. Faked the fact that hostess bars did make me nervous.

"All I'm saying is don't march in asking questions. Be subtle. And I know that place does extras, if you know what I mean."

Lenny swivelled in his chair and drew up the blinds, a multi-coloured light show of the busy junction. Midnight, and it was filled with revellers heading out or tottering into the station, swaying home drunk on the last train or ready to down shots of tequila and party till dawn. Pimps waited by the crossing, petitioned the men into bars and massage parlours. At the police box officers leaned on broom handle truncheons, watching the scene with bored indifference.

"I've truly seen a lot of shit," said Lenny. "Growing up in Chicago, brother shot. Two years in the army fighting motherfuckers at boot camp before I even get to Kuwait. But nothing freakier than here."

Traffic flowed, taxis, cars and bikes, boys on souped-up mopeds weaving between the pedestrians.

"Some people get spooked by the crowds, a rush hour train. You know what gives me the stone cold shits?"

We watched the lights change, the bodies pour across the road.

"An empty street."

**

Mazzy had got into the habit of patrolling the apartment with the Gamma Scout, taking readings in different rooms and recording them on her iPad.

"Is this for your information?" I asked. "Or your mom's?"

"Everybody's," she snapped.

We were fumbling through our morning routine, eating toast and talking to each other across the hallway.

"I put a daily reading on Facebook."

She walked into the kitchen, balancing her screen like a waiter with a tray.

"Are we glowing?"

"I don't know why it doesn't bother you."

When I told her that the background radiation of London or LA exceeded Tokyo she said, "Whatever," and went back to her desk.

I ironed my shirt, tried, and failed, not to think about The Island, the phone call.

Then I went into Mazzy's room and apologised.

"I have to go, dad."

She was brushing her hair in the mirror.

"You're right," I said. "It was good of your mum to mail it over." I sat on the end of the bed, explained to her that there would always be competition for her attention between us, her parents.

She stopped brushing and stared at me as if I'd just told her the Earth was flat. "Dad, you left mom and went back to England."

"It wasn't as simple as that."

"I have to go to school."

She had a grip in her teeth, twisting a braid between her fingers.

"I got pretty good at doing your hair when you were younger."

She sighed, smiled. "What about the photo at Uncle Gavin's? It looks like a plant growing out of my head."

"There was a bit of trial and error, that's true."

She fixed her hair and turned. "Don't you have to go to uni?"

"Sure," I stood up and passed Mazzy her bag. "I could meet you in Shibuya if you want a coffee later?"

"I'm going to karaoke after school."

"With Larissa?"

"And some others. All the kids go here. It's not like a bar, you know."

I told her I understood, that I'd see her later.

"Okay?"

"Okay," I replied, not sure if her 'Okay?' was checking for my permission, or asking after my emotional well-being.

I walked out with Mazzy and gave her a big hug when we parted ways at the station. Then I sat on the platform, waiting for a carriage not jammed with faces pressed against the windows. While I sat on a plastic seat, watching the anonymous lives swallowed by the sliding doors of the next few trains, I was overwhelmed by memory.

In an effort to hold on to what has been, I experimented with my nostalgia, creating a trance like state by meditating on previous events. I could experience a near complete jump of consciousness to a virtual world. A form of mental time travel until I was afraid that opening my eyes would reveal the room, the landscape or the person, that I'd tricked myself into recreating.

Images of Kozue had appeared more visceral than women I was dating in England. If I thought of her, she was there. A physical presence. Sitting on a hotel chair and rolling up a stocking. Zipping her skirt and smoothing out the creases. My brain had become frighteningly adept at recreating the original scene.

Mazzy too.

If I catch a whiff of bleach, or hear the echo of a voice along a tiled hallway, I can stand again in the delivery room and feel the weight of her in my arms. All the cold knowledge of cells and genes undone by the gurgling miracle.

By god, the thought is that startling I could drop her if I'm not careful. I need to focus on the here and now, and let her body flutter away.

二十一

THE POLICE ARRESTED Koji outside the carbonised shell of his grandmother's house, and then released him on bail pending charges of arson. With the last of his father's inheritance he rented a cheap apartment in Tokyo, and on his first night in the bare room he sat and wrote out a list of names. The Leader. His high school PE teacher. The detective who smirked when he told them about his grandmother's ghost.

Often he walked the entertainment districts, Roppongi and Kabuki-cho. Sometimes he followed foreign women home, but no further than their apartment doors. Once his money ran out he worked for a shipping company in Nishi-Nippori. He signed forms and checked boxes. He walked through warehouses stacked with sea containers. The reek of salt and fish. Vacant, rotting days. Offset by the buzz of imported pornography.

One morning he caught a train over to the old group house, the boarded up windows and Keep Out signs. He walked across the overgrown garden and peered through the letterbox. A litter of post in the empty hallway, a pile of grubby sheets. The thought of her walking, drifting the corridors in her white yukata. Koji, the chosen one, a step behind.

He found out she was dead in an email. Etsuko had decided that Koji should know she died in a bed surrounded by her true family. She also told him how they saw a white cat in the hospital car park.

Koji felt nothing at the news. Perhaps a mild disappointment, his calculated justice not realised.

That night he hired a Bulgarian stripper to undress in a windowless brothel.

He began to budget his salary around paying for sex. He could forget himself with the foreign prostitutes. In a basement parlour with a pale skinned whore he was the master of his paltry existence. The naked women who took him from his own body, the despicable flesh and blood of his father.

Still, it was never enough. And there was ambition in his fetish, his soma. He saved his wages and bought a ticket to Los Angeles for no other reason than this was where the inflated models fucked and contorted on his pixel screen.

He felt small arriving in the USA. A boy in a man's world. Then along the sun bleached boardwalks he saw the peroxide women. He took photos. He went to strip clubs. He watched the Americans slip dollar bills into stocking tops and did the same. In the afternoons he learned to speak English at a language school. He was obsessive about grammar, and twice changed teacher when he noted colloquialisms that weren't in his dictionary.

He was also obsessive about paying for women to visit his hotel. Pale and blonde. Then the escort agencies refused to send out girls to his room, and two men arrived at his door instead of the woman he'd requested. One of them tied him to a chair while the other stole money from his suitcase. Then they whipped him with a plug flex.

He flew back to Tokyo, the open wounds seeping through his shirt and staining the seat cover.

Within months he'd saved his wages and travelled back to Los Angeles. Again calling on the services of the escort agencies. He had fantasies about torturing the pimps. Scenes from bad action films where they begged him for mercy. But they never returned. Whatever happened between Koji and the rented women.

Then there was an accident. The girl left a trail of blood across the sheets, on the shower curtain and out onto the motel landing. Like a thread of wool to find the way home. Koji had shut the door behind her, taken off his belt and fixed it to the light fitting. When he kicked away the chair the ceiling collapsed and left him on the floor covered in plaster.

That same night he boarded the plane for Tokyo, and sat beside her.

She was too precious for this world.

Luckily he was there to protect her. To watch over her. He wondered if he might be some kind of guardian, assigned to her care. Redeemed.

二十二

I TRIED TO look younger. I shaved and bought designer clothes, a pot of styling wax. When I got back from university Mazzy was still at karaoke with her friends, and I went into my room and slipped on my new shirt. I stuck a handful of wax in my hair and sucked in my stomach, checking my profile in the mirror.

Perhaps Lenny was right. The simulation was an archive. Part of the memory with Kozue was bound in the self I was then. Not now. From the moment I'd seen her in Hiroshima I'd warped from the ashamed father, the self regulated logician, to a bewitched man attracted to a mystery woman.

When Mazzy came home I quickly pushed my door to and towelled the wax from my hair, pulled off my new shirt and called back a hello.

"Can we eat nabe again?" she shouted from the hallway.

"Good idea."

"I'm starving."

I was glad she wanted to spend time with me, that I had distraction from the jittery stage fright thinking about a trip to the hostess club.

While Mazzy got changed I counted my spare cash. Sixty grand. Equivalent to five hundred quid with the steroidal yen against the weakling pound. Still, it might not be enough.

"Do I need my purse, dad?"

"Don't be silly." I pulled another credit card from the drawer and slipped it into my wallet.

We jumped on the train to Ginza and walked the wide avenue, ogling price tags in the flagship stores. Here, the Tokyo rich paraded their wealth. The ostentatious bags dangled as signs of a superior solvency, a class marker. The perfect accompaniment to the money show was a super car rally touring the streets. Engines revved and backfired, and the shoppers came out of luxury department stores to photograph spoilers and chrome.

After watching the cars and crowds I took Mazzy to a nabe restaurant where patrons sat around a circular, copper counter, and dipped strips of meat into simmering water.

"This is so cool," said Mazzy. "Cooking your own food."

Just as I'd hoped, the dining style matched her strident independence. We dunked vegetables, pork and beef, before draping them in sesame sauce.

"Do you remember grilling your own fish in Greece? You wouldn't eat one unless you could do it yourself."

"We had a barbecue on that sandbank."

"That was great holiday."

"Corfu?"

"And that day we went snorkelling."

"God. You want to remember that?"

I'd trodden on a sea urchin, the black spines snapping off in my sole. In utter agony, I'd collapsed on a rock and wondered how the hell we were going to get back to the hotel. Then my nine year old daughter lifted up my foot and calmly removed the poisonous spines, one by one with her delicate fingers, as if she were a journeyman medic field dressing a wounded soldier.

"I was thinking more of that shoal we swam into."

Taking her into the sea, and not being terrified of the consequences, was cognitive therapy towards reducing my constant anxiety about her safety. Mazzy was fearless, and had no memory of her near drowning. She was a natural in the water, like her mother, but for years I avoided taking her anywhere near a beach. Then we put on masks and flippers and snorkelled the turquoise bays, hovered in the rays of subaquatic sun.

And here she was in Tokyo, young and thriving. Her own woman.

Once we left the nabe restaurant and decided to head back, it was Mazzy who flagged down the cab and asked for the apartment, instructing the driver how to get us home.

**

I walked up to Roppongi after midnight, the two beers I drank engendering a false bravado. Still, I needed another hit before walking into a hostess club and had a shot in Wall Street, a narrow, rowdy bar, filled with a mix of expats and locals, from the loud-mouth traders with foreign banks to the drunken students leftover from happy hour. I sat at the counter and looked around the room, imagined them a clientèle banished from the light of day. Then I ordered a double whisky, downed it, and left.

I stepped off the main drag and followed Lenny's sketched map around the back streets, turning the crude drawing in my hand to follow his directions. I walked past a gang of mangy cats, two Thai transsexuals who giggled and pouted, before I came to the building that housed The Island. A thin block with a bar on each floor. Some of the clubs had pictures of the hostesses who worked there, profiles of doe-eyed girls with dyed hair and bright make up. The plastic sign for The Island was a silver palm tree and a bikinied woman leaning against the trunk.

After stepping into the lift I took my wallet from my coat and slipped it into my trouser pocket. My heart beat faster. From here in it was possible I could see Kozue.

The doors opened and a skinny Japanese man with a white shirt and black waistcoat stepped forward and welcomed me into the lobby. In carefully rehearsed English he asked if I could speak Japanese and was noticeably relieved when I answered that I could. He showed me to the cloakroom and deftly took my jacket, before leading me along a walkway that bridged a miniature stream dotted with tropical fish.

I expected something tawdrier than the lacquered surfaces and low lighting of the main club. A large, curved bar was kept by a tall and dark Caucasian guy, possibly Balkan or Eastern European, and the high-backed, semi-circular booth seats were candlelit as if fanned shells illuminated by a shining pearl.

"*Konbanwa*," welcomed the beehived and sequinned manageress. She spoke in a husky, tobacco drawl. A woman who'd spent most of her life with a cigarette pinched between her lips.

We exchanged bows, and she beckoned over two women from stools at the counter. Both hostesses seemed entirely constructed of heels and legs, floating smiles and fake eyelashes. Despite the cigarette smoke filling the room, the sweet perfume of my two courtesans emanated, and until we sat down at a table I was briefly lost as to why I was there – the reptilian brain alive and well in the measured academic.

Mayumi was in her thirties, but had made herself up to be mid twenties. She'd scraped back her shining hair, and wore large gold earrings that dangled over her bare shoulders. Akemi was younger, sporting a short, platinum dyed bob, and large eyes with glittery make up dusted over her cheeks. She wasn't as confident as Mayumi, and probably a lower rank, such is the organisation of even a hostess bar in Japan, as she took our drink order of three glasses of sparkling wine, which immediately set me back ten thousand yen.

The ladies sat either side of me, two sets of naked thighs, skirt hems skilfully adjusted. When the drinks arrived, possibly the worst glass of watered down vinegar I've ever tasted, they asked the Japanese standards: Where was I from? How long had I been here? Did I like Japanese food? The women?

I answered, smiled, told a few unimportant lies and scanned the other hostesses working the room. Mostly Japanese, similarly dolled up and posturing, pouring drinks and resting hands, each and every gesture as if a line from a script. There was a pair of blonde foreigners at the corner table, drinking champagne with a younger Japanese man who dressed and held himself with the manner of entitlement. Either the heir to a wealthy family, or the lineage of a yakuza boss.

Kozue wasn't here. And looking around it was hard to imagine her part of the scene.

"You don't like Japanese girl?" asked Mayumi in English, put out I wasn't giving her the attention I was paying for. "You want Russian lady?"

I told her of course not, and flattered them both with hollow compliments. I ordered another round of drinks, and even smoked a cigarette when offered and lit by Akemi. The more I indulged them, and myself, the sooner I'd earn the right to ask questions about Kozue. To enhance my status as a patron worthy of their time and effort I embellished my earning power, bragged that the strength of the yen had made me rich.

When the bottle of champagne arrived in a bucket of ice, Akemi's hand was on my knee and Mayumi's bare thigh rested against my leg. I insisted on pouring the first drinks from the bottle, getting cheap giggles from the 'English gentleman' stereotype. We touched glasses and drank, eye contact lingering, the gestures less subtle now. From the palm on my leg to the footsie under the table. I was getting drunk, but could do little about it as with each sip Akemi would top up my glass. But this did mean I was getting braver about asking after Kozue, and was going to attempt a question when a karaoke mic started the rounds. We endured a tuneless croak from a sweating businessman, still in his crumpled work shirt and cheap suit, no doubt making the most of a company account, before one of the Russian girls stood up and sang a passable version of 'You're So Vain.'

After the hostess finished the song she was applauded and returned to her sharply dressed customer. She sat down slightly apart from him, and he reached out and grabbed her arm, drunkenly pulling her closer before running his hands through her blonde hair with more disdain than admiration. He then leaned over and whispered something in her ear, before calling over the mama-san who took them through a mirrored door to another room.

"You want to go to a karaoke booth?" asked Mayumi, hooking her hand around the inside of my thigh. "Akemi can come as well."

Akemi nodded, smiled. "I can dance for you."

I leaned over and grabbed my glass as if it were a life ring.

I thought about the photo of Richard Feynman in Las Vegas, surrounded by feathered showgirls. The brilliant physicist indulging his testosterone. Then I drank, balancing the dichotomy between brain and body.

"Next time," I said, totting up my bill. I calculated that I was one drink away from sixty thousand yen, and moved to make sure I left the club with a lead on Kozue if I was going to spend over five hundred quid.

Casually, or so I believed, I asked Mayumi how long she'd been working here. She ummed and ahhed, before guessing about a year.

I nodded, feigned my buzz of hearing potential information. I drank again, and instead of devising some wily discourse, I clumsily asked if she knew Kozue.

"Kozue," she repeated, raising her eyebrows and lighting a cigarette. "Girls come and go."

"Tall," I said. "From Hiroshima."

There was a flash of recognition, the mask briefly pulled aside before she returned to hostessing.

I'd driven into a dead end, and she was watching me slowly reverse out. "I used to go to a club in Hiroshima," I lied. "She worked there, and I heard she came here."

Mayumi nodded. She told Akemi to pour me a drink.

"Perhaps you know her?"

"Hundreds of girls have worked here," she said. "I don't know them all." She shrugged her shoulders and took a deep inhale of her cigarette.

Akemi poured the last few drops of flat champagne into my glass. I drank, watched a man paw a girl's knee across the room, and then checked my watch and abruptly told them it was time for me to leave.

After a chorus of, "So soon," and, "Why don't we have another bottle of champagne," I was shown to the bar where I settled my bill, fifty eight thousand yen, including the most expensive bowl of peanuts I've ever eaten.

The women escorted me to the cloakroom and stood in the lobby while we waited for the lift. As the doors pinged open Mayumi said, "Next time you come, maybe I'll remember more about Kozue."

Then I stepped into the lift. Both women bowing and waving as the doors closed, any machinations from Mayumi well hidden behind a wide, lipstick smile.

Descending to the ground floor, I imagined Kozue working the room, pouring drinks and nodding, bored, slipping away on visions of hills and frosted trees, painting the moon on an autumn lake.

**

It was 5am when I left The Island, but the neon still burned against the cold. I saw a whole street filled with bulbs and void of people. SANYO. FUJI. KONICA. COKE. Dazzling brands in the after world. How rare to have Tokyo to oneself. For the briefest second I had the fear that Lenny had, that I was the last man alive walking the abandoned city.

Then I turned onto Roppongi dori. There were girls going home from clubs and bars, smudges of make-up and balancing heels. Pimps shuffled in doorways, stamped their feet and rubbed their hands, hoping to lure drunken stragglers from the winter chill to a subterranean warmth. Flesh and sex, empty wallets.

I was prey. The lone white man at the end of the night. I brushed off grubby deals on blowjobs and massage, a discount involving two Brazilian girls. I'd almost run the gauntlet when a Nigerian began a different kind of pitch.

"I see you," he said. "You're a smart guy, I know. But you think too much. Take a rest, brother."

I broke my stare and looked over. Parallel scars across his cheeks, a thin moustache that moved as if a separate entity to the rest of his face.

"You know what I know. The universe expanding. Rock and

ice. Bits of dust. Dead planets. You too, brother. We made of stars, but we cold and lonely. Strange, no? Strange, yes. Because we don't need to be shivering, brother. And we both know where we're never cold."

I tried to ignore him, but turned to his nodding, smiling face.

"A pussy, brother. All the heat of the sun between a woman's legs. We spend nine months trying to get out of it, realise the world is a cold, cold mother, and then spend the rest of our life trying to get back in."

He grabbed my shoulder and turned me around. "A good fuck, brother. Whether you pay for it or not. Because time stops, and the universe is no bigger than your dick."

I swore at him and crossed over the road.

"I see you," he shouted. "Dust, brother. You're no better than me."

I walked a little more briskly, and then jogged.

**

"Did you have insomnia or something?"

Mazzy slopped across the kitchen in her slippers and swung open the fridge door.

"Insomnia?"

"This morning," she said. "Like 5am or something. I heard you walking around."

"I couldn't sleep."

"Which is the low fat again?" She was holding up two cartons, thankfully more interested in which milk was low calorie, and not what her father had been up to the night before.

"The one with the cow on."

She sat down at the table and poured out a bowl of granola. "You don't look like you did."

"Look like what?"

"You slept."

"A few hours."

Mazzy crunched a mouthful of berries and nuts, and then reached over the table for the coffee.

"Were you drinking?"

"What?"

I'd had a shower, but the vinegary champagne was seeping from my pores.

"I thought it would help me sleep."

"Help you smell."

She poured her coffee and spooned in the sugar. I knew she was studying me so avoided her eyes and read the paper.

I met Yamada in the canteen that afternoon. I was definitely hungover, and perhaps he too smelled the alcohol, because he suggested we visit his local bathhouse in Ikegami.

"The water is black, volcanic. Straight from earth's core."

A soul rejuvenating *sento,* washed clean by a spring heated in the broken mantle. It was the perfect tonic to a night out. After a stressful research session watching Russians argue with each other about the most efficient way to cut fifty equilateral triangles in under two minutes, I jammed onto the Yamanote line towards Shinagawa. Whatever aggrandised vision I had of myself, on a rush hour train I was just another commuter bumping through the city. Oblivious to the life beside me, the heat of an unknown body pressed upon my flesh. Yet close enough to feel a heartbeat, a pulse, more intimate than a bad day with an indifferent lover.

By the time I got to Ikegami I was more than ready for a soak and a scrub, to resurrect myself from a Japanese bath. I met Yamada at the station and we walked along suburban back streets to a rather unremarkable looking entrance at the bottom of an apartment block.

"Wait till you see the water," said Yamada, slipping off his shoes and placing them in a wooden locker. "Even the most luxurious spa doesn't have the atmosphere of a community bathhouse."

I parted the door curtain and paid the mama-san. We went through to the changing rooms where naked men sat cooling after their scalding baths.

The moment one enters a sento, time begins to drip. Old and wrinkled bodies wobbled from the steam room to sit on plastic stools, washing and scrubbing before dipping that tentative little toe. The rhythm of sloshing water poured over heads lathered with soap, echoed about the tiles. A wall divided the male and female section of a bathhouse, and as we washed I could hear women and children chatting on the other side.

"*Kimochi*," said Yamada, pouring water over his shoulders.

It did feel good, the only focus our unfettered bodies.

Yamada looked around the sento, the unadorned. "*Skinship*, *ne*."

Skinship, the Japanese term for bonding through communal nakedness, the belief that nudity with your neighbours strengthens local relationships. Watching these private rituals of cleansing unveiled, and noting the absolute lack of shyness in a culture that is notoriously shy, there was a definite *funiki,* an atmosphere of collective bathers rather than individuals. While many English still shudder at the thought of being naked in front of friends or family, the apes we have descended from still bathe in groups. Famously the monkey troupes of northern Japan sit in heated pools while snow settles on their heads in icy crowns. Like the cats who decided to stay cats, the monkeys knew well enough not to climb from the water and start wearing clothes.

After scrubbing with soap and a pumice stone, a dip in the simmering jacuzzi, Yamada stepped into the black depths of the volcanic bath.

I put my hand in the oily darkness, watched my fingers vanish. Yamada submerged up to his neck, eyes closed. I followed him into the molten water, each white limb consumed by the dark sump. Then I sat and melted, lost the day and its petty dramas.

I nearly fainted climbing out, but a dousing of cold water brought me round and we sat on a bench in the changing room, my whole body thudding like a giant heart.

"We forget the skin is an organ." Yamada lowered his mouth to the drinking fountain.

I floated into my clothes, adrift on a post-bath haze, and the jazz muzak, a plaintive saxophone that reverberated around the wooden panels.

We ambled back to Yamada's along the quiet streets, a full moon with a munificent face floating above the city as if observing its own creation. Silver tiles on a temple roof, power lines looped from pole to pole like spider silk. We passed a cat sitting on a wall, basking in the lunar splendour as if an acolyte called to worship. The whole scene was a fanciful sketch, but here it was in perfect vision. The moon a master artist, and us the fortuitous subjects.

Only when we left the residential streets and came onto the busy road towards Omori, did we need to begin a conversation.

"How's Mazzy settling in?"

"She loves it."

Yamada nodded, smiled. "The *gaijin* honeymoon period."

"Mine has never ended."

"Happily married to Japan?"

Perhaps it was the surging afterglow of a volcanic bath. But I did, briefly, entertain the far-fetched idea of finding Kozue and falling in love again. That I lived in a house like Yamada's. No, that in fact I lived in Yamada's house, and Mazzy would come and stay and look after our children and fall for Kozue, like I had. And in this fairy tale vision of our shining future the full moon gleamed like mercury every blessed night.

**

I thought the cleansing sento had washed away the base desire, and that the walk back along the quiet streets had revealed the moonlit fantasy.

"Next time you come, maybe I'll remember more about Kozue."

However, Mayumi's words had followed me from The Island. That week at university, either in meetings with my assistants, or setting tasks for our guinea pigs, or when I was at home chatting with Mazzy, the world was enough. Content in my progress, both professional and paternal.

Then I'd get on the train and think of Kozue. The need to find out had become a fever, a sickness that only she could cure.

I resolved to make one last trip to The Island. If nothing came of it I'd end my search for a woman I'd only met a handful of times. This was the logical course of action. I sat with my notebook and wrote down the pros and cons of the quest. Positives included my own closure, or falling in love again when I'd pretty much given up on the idea. The cons were disrupting an exalted memory, upsetting Mazzy, or pushing into what might be a settled life for Kozue. Perhaps I'd discover a terrible truth that I was somehow responsible for or could do nothing to help.

I was still jotting down my thoughts when Mazzy came in late, tired.

"Do you have to watch TV so loud?"

There was a sumo basho on that I was barely following.

"And a good evening to you?"

I snapped shut my notebook. When she tried to shrug off her backpack it caught on her sleeve, and she wriggled violently before swearing and unzipping her coat to let it all drop to the hallway floor.

"Fuck."

"Mazzy."

She kicked off her shoes and came into the lounge.

"I'm guessing a bad day?" I switched off the TV and asked her what was wrong.

"Nothing."

"Yes there is."

"Shoot me if I go to Baskin Robbins again."

"The ice cream place?"

She shook her head. Her skin looked puffy, hair greasy. Although I guessed she was pre-menstrual, I certainly wasn't going to mention my observation. Once a month her mother was capable of murder, and Mazzy had inherited this hormonally powered rage that no words or actions could quell.

"All I wanted was nuts instead of hundreds and thousands. How hard is that?"

"A nut problem?"

"It's not funny. You should be studying this shit." She swung open the fridge door and grabbed the block of cheese and cut off a slice. "If I knew how to say it in Japanese, I would have."

"Say what?"

"That genocide can only happen when people like her follow orders."

I told her to sit down and talk to me properly. Once she'd filled a bowl with nachos and grated cheese and microwaved it all into a yellow coagulation topped with salsa and a dollop of sour cream, she slouched on the sofa. Legs dangled over the arm, she lifted handfuls of goop to her mouth between telling the story of how she wanted an ice cream sundae slightly different to the menu, and that despite the box of nuts next to the server's hand any variation from the standard order was, "*Muri.*"

"Impossible."

"All she had to do was sprinkle some fucking nuts on the top."

Instead of explaining that an unswerving compliance to rules, whether social codes or the stipulations of chain restaurants, delivered trains on time and cheap ice cream, I said, "That is fucked."

Mazzy laughed, and then told me off for swearing before complaining that eating an entire bowl of nachos had made her feel sick.

And just as I would've done with her mother, I told her I'd run a bath.

She said, "Thanks, dad," and checked her buzzing phone. "Mom says, 'Hi'."

"That's funny."

"Funny?"

"I was just thinking of her."

"Weird." She glanced up, a look I thought was a question.

"Nothing."

"Nothing what?"

I cut short the exchange. Lydia was in the apartment enough already. Whether it was her voice beamed along a fibre optic cable, or her authority in the daily radiation count and what foods to avoid, she was here.

I went into the bathroom and set the temperature, sitting on the edge of the tub and watching water gush from the faucet.

"Bubbles, dad," shouted Mazzy. "I want a proper bath."

I poured in the soap and stirred with my hand. My heart thumping at the vision. Terrified to see her, right there. Kozue. Wet and gleaming. That dark, swirling hair, floating around her like the serpents of Medusa.

二十三

MAZZY WOKE UP needing the bathroom. Mouth dry from a bowl of salted chips, the dull ache of sleeping with a full bladder.

What was the time?

She felt around for her phone, couldn't find it. Then she got out of bed and stepped into the hallway. Her father was in the lavatory, his bedroom door ajar. Laid on his desk was a brand new shirt, his wallet, and a spread of ten thousand yen bills. Mazzy noted the opened pot of styling wax on the dresser just before she heard the latch. Although she had no reason to dart back into her room, she did, waiting behind her door in breath-held silence, listening.

Each of her father's actions had that deliberate effort to be quiet, and in this effort each sound was all the more conspicuous. She barely heard his bedroom door close. In a flash she was under her covers, feigning sleep.

Five minutes later she listened to her own door brush across the carpet. She remembered pretending to be asleep when she was little, when her father would sit in her room and watch her. She'd tell him that she was okay, that there weren't any monsters in her closet.

Again, still, he was checking she was in bed.

On hearing the front door click shut, she threw back the covers and pulled on her jeans. She grabbed a hat and a coat and jumped into her shoes, and went out onto the landing. The elevator was descending to the ground floor. Before she hit the call button she imagined the horror if he forgot something and she was standing there when he stepped out. She skipped down the stairwell and bumped open the fire exit, in case the concierge was still on duty.

She watched her father turn from the driveway, then followed him onto the street. If he got in a taxi, she decided, she wasn't hailing the car behind and uttering the clichéd words. That was beyond curiosity. Insane.

But he didn't. He walked briskly towards the Azabu crossing, under the elevated highway, and up the hill. Mazzy followed from the opposite side of the road, daring herself to get closer. The streets were quiet, but not empty. A wedding party gathered outside a restaurant, friends posed for pictures with the bride. And of course there were the drunken salarymen in crumpled suits swinging cheap briefcases, there always were.

Until her father neared Roppongi the pursuit was fun. Then there were women in doorways. Chinese women, Mazzy guessed, in leather boots and quilted ski jackets, beckoning men downstairs to a basement brothel. They petitioned the night owls, "*Massage ikaga desu ka?*" and stared at her when she walked past. She'd been entertaining the thought that her father was on a date, and that she might spy on their rendezvous, and how that would be enough for her to go home feeling satisfied, rather than guilty, for following him.

Now she feared that she'd watch him descend one of these staircases. What then? But he walked past the prostitutes and took the backstreet that looped by the Hard Rock Cafe onto Roppongi dori. She might have followed him further, but two men eating kebabs called out to her.

"Hello darling," said one man, spilling salad down his shirt.

"Please, marriage," said the other.

It was dark, and two shadows were shouting at her.

She turned and headed home. Fear and shame. The thought that she wasn't ready for the world, and that she needed to do something about it.

二十四

KOJI DIDN'T FOLLOW her father. He already knew where he was going. He'd followed him before, all the way to the door of a hostess club. Another foreign pig crushing a Japanese flower.

Koji watched him turn up the hill towards Roppongi, and then he stepped from the doorway so he could see the reception, the concierge. Forever on guard. Koji had noted his shifts, that he hadn't taken a day off in three weeks. Company man. No movement unless it was written in the company guidebook. Koji knew where he lived, had seen his one room apartment. In this dutiful employee he saw his old, pathetic self. A man who only acted on the will of another.

Now Koji was the auteur of his own fate.

And hers.

He was waiting for the concierge to leave the counter. He knew he had menial tasks to complete, taking out the garbage or checking the laundry. Koji planned to walk through the empty foyer and up the staircase, all the way to her apartment.

Then she threw open the fire exit doors and jogged down the driveway, zipping up her jacket.

Koji ducked behind the gate and waited for her to go by. Then he followed. His stomach cartwheeling. The three of them heading towards the Roppongi neon. Koji wanted her to know what he did about her father. That he paid for sex. That he left his daughter alone to haunt the rooms of puppet women.

There were no saints.

She could see her father, and Koji could see her. They went past restaurants and bars, tables lit with candles and hollow chatter. Waxen faces, melting. Your life is what you remember. Koji could recall every second of his existence since the flight from Los Angeles.

She was on the dark street behind Roppongi dori, near the

pool hall, when two foreign men shouted across the road. Leered and cat-called. Scared, she turned and walked away, hurrying back to the apartment, as Koji reached into his pocket for the sharp metal.

二十五

I WALKED INTO The Island, two hours after the vision of Kozue in the bath.

"*Konbanwa*, Ben san."

I hadn't even told the Japanese doorman my name, and he knew who I was.

"*Dozo*," he waved me towards the cloakroom. Once again, his ghost touch slipping the jacket from my shoulders.

Then the mama-san appeared, as if materialised from a haze of cigarette smoke. She wore a navy blue dress covered in sequins, and her glittered attire matched the sparkle of her smile.

I looked around the club for Mayumi. Before I could request her the mama-san had called two other women from the counter. Akemi, the champagne pourer from my last visit, and another woman called Kaori, a buxom and flouncy hostess, who immediately led us over to a table, her breast tactically pressed against my arm.

When I got the menu, and again read the extravagant price of the drinks, I asked Akemi to call over the mama-san.

"*Daijobu?*" asked Kaori.

"Mayumi, *mitai*," said Akemi, sitting back, making little attempt to hide a feeling of rejection.

The mama-san came over, and asked if everything was to my liking. Of course, I'd shown my cards, the reason I was here. In protracted Japanese she explained that Mayumi was unavailable but 'probably' available if I wanted to sing karaoke with her in the private room.

"Kaori and Akemi can join you until she's free."

I nodded, and wondered what kind of billing would come up on my credit card statement for the 'Extras.'

The ladies escorted me through the club area towards the back.

I took surreptitious glances as we walked, scanning the tables. The only face I caught eyes with was the Japanese man I'd seen with the blonde Russians. He was leant back in the seat, twirling a coin along his fingers like a magician, seemingly bored, or angered, by the woman beside him.

Mayumi.

I'd requested his hostess. Great. My second visit here and I was annoying the resident mobster.

I looked away from his cold stare and pushed open the door to our lounge, a low lit den of a room, with a large leather sofa, a karaoke screen in the corner and two microphones on the coffee table.

Kaori sang first, a Japanese number about sun and love. Either she was drunk, or quite possibly on cocaine, as she had that hyperactivity and jerky concentration that blockading the dopamine transmitter inevitably causes. While she pranced and wailed, Akemi slipped her hand around my waist.

This was not what I'd come for. Each time I asked about Mayumi, I was told, "Soon," and encouraged to order another round of drinks. After a melody of Japanese pop and a Beatles favourite, which I'd only sung so Kaori didn't caterwaul again, the ladies abruptly stood. Mayumi was at the door with another woman, Yuki, a feline beauty who seemed barely old enough to be working as a hostess.

Mayumi was all smiles, as was Yuki, the two of them taking a seat either side of me. I ordered what I hoped would be my last ever round of drinks at this money pit, and tipsily sang *Light My Fire*, the karaoke standard I'd once crooned for Kozue in Hiroshima.

I was applauded, and certainly expected to be if I was financing my own fan base. Then I sat down and got on with the business of finding out if Mayumi knew anything or not.

"After you left, I remembered her." She lit a cigarette, took a breath and blew out a stream of violet smoke, with no hurry to tell me anything in a room that charged by the hour. "And I realised that Yuki and her had been good friends."

I looked over to Yuki. Her blue contacts glowed. Despite her youth she already seemed to have the guile of an experienced companion.

"Is she still a hostess?"

Yuki smiled, shook her head. "Even if you finish working, you're always a hostess."

Mayumi laughed, agreed. "What man doesn't need his ego massaged."

They giggled together, and then supposed too that I was one of these men, and quickly replaced their hands on my knees.

We drank and sang some more. Before I had to order another refill I tried for details on Kozue, and asked Yuki if they kept in touch.

"I think I have her number." She sipped her champagne. "In my old phone."

"But we can't give out numbers," said Mayumi.

"*Sou desu ne*," agreed Yuki.

"Not in here, anyway."

The women looked to each other, the telepathy of hostessing. Yuki said, "You can have my number though, and maybe we can meet. Outside The Island."

Progress. I thought. Yuki took an eye-liner pencil from her purse, wrote her number on the back of a receipt and tucked it into my shirt pocket. "I like yakitori if you want to take me somewhere."

Mayumi sang one more song, an unexpectedly moving *enka* number about a woman who falls in love with a kamikaze pilot. Then I made a move to pay my bill. Once again I walked past the surly Japanese patron at the corner table. Unnervingly, he watched me through the smoke. Like a man who knew the last thought in my head as I dropped off to sleep each night.

While the mama-san totted up my bill, I asked Mayumi about her friend.

"Who?"

"The Japanese guy you were sitting with."

"Oh, just a regular, that's all." She shrugged her shoulders, passed off my question. I didn't need Lenny's body language skills to know he was more than that.

When I looked up from signing the receipt, Yuki was sliding on to the chair beside him. She nodded and poured his drink, and then leant over to light his cigarette.

二十六

THE MORNING AFTER Mazzy followed her father into Roppongi she checked his room as if she were his mother, not his daughter. His clothes piled on the floor. Notes and coins scattered across his desk. He woke up and caught her peeking in, and she quickly said she'd make him breakfast.

"What a treat."

She studied him sitting up in bed, examined his face for details of the previous evening.

"Okay?"

"You want French toast?"

"Perfect."

She made him French toast and they sat at the kitchen table and drank coffee. She knew something about him now, but she wasn't sure what it was. So they ate breakfast and listened to the radio. He only looked up from the paper when there was news about a stabbing in Roppongi, two Belgian men, one in critical condition.

"The only dodgy place in the country," he said. "I don't want you going out there."

She was embarrassed by what she knew.

"Ever."

By his warning.

"Okay."

"Even in the daytime."

So I don't catch you there? That's what she wanted to say. It was all she could think about for the next three days, whether she was on the train to school or daydreaming in class.

二十七

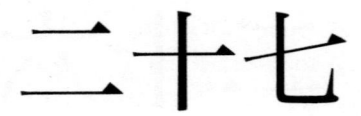

THREE NIGHTS AFTER Yuki popped her phone number into my pocket, I took her for a drink beyond the mirrored walls of The Island.

We met in a smoky izakaya under the arches at Yurakacho, one of the drinking dens burrowed into the brickwork beneath the train tracks. There were booth seats at the back, where I could sit and see the rest of the bar, who was coming through the door.

When Yuki did arrive, perfumed and mini-skirted, I was glad the shadows kept the watching eyes from us. Although the Japanese customers barely noticed a man with a woman half his age, I knew that other foreigners would see through my chest with x-ray vision, my hollow heart.

She sat in the seat by my side rather than across the table, a knee immediately resting against my leg. I began the evening like a social worker, asking concerned questions about her family, how she got into hostessing. When I asked what part of Japan she was from, she said, "All over," and told me that after catching her mother reading her diary she'd ripped out the pages and burned them.

And then she left home and ran away to work in a nightclub.

"Tokyo is the best city in Japan." She pushed away the mugs of icy beer I'd ordered and asked for a glass of rum and coke.

I ordered a new drink, along with skewers of chicken parts, and began the pursuit for Kozue, asking Yuki if she'd seen her recently.

"Hmm, not for a while."

Yuki downed her rum and coke, and then ordered another from the passing waiter. As she hadn't really answered my direct question, I made some idle chit chat about karaoke songs and food. It was tough going, so I brought the conversation back to Kozue.

"Do you know if she's married?"

Yuki shrugged her shoulders. She grabbed a skewer and pulled off a glazed spring onion with her teeth. Above our heads another train shuttled along the rails, vibrating the light fittings and rippling the beer in my glass.

"I think she's retired from hostessing."

Her blue contacts had the aquamarine of a swimming pool, and I had to keep myself from thinking that it wasn't just the lenses that were fake.

"Do you have her number?"

She shook her head. "Maybe. I couldn't find my old phone."

I wondered if she'd even met Kozue. A blunt interrogation would get me nowhere, so I told her that her blue contacts suited her, and then asked more about the diary.

"What exactly did you burn?"

She smiled, narrowed her eyes, and again became that feline hostess. "*Sekkusu.*"

I took a skewer and chewed gristly meat, forcing down a rubbery mouthful before I asked Yuki what I was eating.

"Chicken skin."

I put the half finished skewer back on the plate. Before I snapped at the lack of information, Yuki sensed her moment. "I know where she lives, though."

Instead of clumsily jumping on this news, I held back the tingling thought of walking up to Kozue's house and knocking on the door. I flirted with Yuki. I indulged her vanities, hair and clothes, and after a couple more beers she said we should go somewhere and relax.

When she ran a hand along my thigh, I knew I had to backtrack from going to a love hotel, and lifted away her palm.

"You don't like me," she sulked. "I want someone to hold." She finished another rum and coke, and pushed the empty glass across the table.

After settling the bill, we walked outside and I hailed a taxi to Shibuya. Yuki made one last attempt to get me into a love hotel, saying that she could massage my shoulders if I was stressed, and that she knew 'special tricks.' When I said, "Next time," she abruptly jumped out of the cab and stomped up the hill.

I quickly paid the driver and caught her up. She said, "If you're not going to be company, then you have to buy me some."

Well aware of the spectacle we were creating, I trailed her clip-clopping heels along the narrow alleys off the main road. I put my hand on her shoulder. I apologised. She stuck out her bottom lip, then took my sleeve and marched us to a pet shop. The window was crowded with toy-sized dogs in plastic pens. Chihuahuas and Dachshunds, yipping and wrestling with cuddly toys.

"Maybe if I had a pet, a cute dog, I'd be less lonely."

I had a feeling where this was going. And so be it, the means to an end. If I wasn't paying for sex, I was paying for a puppy. I knew the scam, that the puppy I bought would be returned to the shop later, and the refund pocketed by Yuki.

She tapped on the glass of a chocolate brown poodle. Tongue and tail wagging, it reared up and begged for release. The pet shop worker swiftly read the situation, the *gaijin* and his rented girl, and sprung the poodle into Yuki's arms. The dog licked her face and trembled with excitement.

"How cute. *Kawaii*. I want her. It is a her?"

The staff member would've snipped it there and then if it had clinched the sale.

Before whipping out my credit card I pulled Yuki and the puppy aside. "If I buy the dog, next time we meet Kozue."

Yuki looked up and studied my face. A serious thought made her appear years beyond her age, not a young woman juggling a poodle.

"*Daijobu*," she said. "I'll take you, don't worry."

I put Yuki and the dog into a taxi, and then waved them off into the night. I pictured the dog watching the city through the window, dumb, helpless, before the taxi looped back around to the pet shop and it was shut back into its plastic box.

二十八

INSTEAD OF REVISING for an exam Mazzy had sung herself hoarse in a Shibuya karaoke box, sharing a peach chu-hai with Larissa that Legolas had ordered, the barman equating height with age and not challenging him for ID.

Mazzy had drunk before, at a sleepover in San Diego. Watching the harbour lights wobble as if she were standing on the deck of a ship. This time she felt giggly and light-headed, not ready to go home and feed her father information about the evening.

After parting with Larissa and Legolas at the ticket barrier she wandered the sodium lit parades, the subterranean warrens of bars and restaurants, the record stores and book shops, the Don Quixote store with its rows of sex toys shelved next to teddy bears and Hello Kitty slippers. There and then, she decided to challenge her father on his midnight escapade to Roppongi. What was he up to sneaking out of the house?

However, her first question would be about that very night in Shibuya.

About the high-heeled girl jumping from a taxi in stalled traffic, leaving the door wide open.

How he got out of the very same car.

Her father.

Mazzy had stood on the pavement and watched, unsure of what she was witnessing. The giraffe-like gait of him striding between the cars. How he caught the girl and put his hand on her shoulder.

"What the fuck?"

She said the words out loud. And meant them. She followed him through the crowds, up the hill past noodle shops and hair salons, before turning onto the back streets. Love hotels, garbage bins from restaurants. She was that close she could hear him talking to her in Japanese.

She wanted to go up and take his hand off her shoulder. Or she wanted to punch him in the face. She wasn't sure which.

She was definitely going to *do something* when they went into a pet shop. Toy-sized dogs jumped around in plastic boxes in the window. Mazzy hid behind a vending machine and watched the girl take out a puppy and cradle it like a baby. Then she watched her father talk to the girl, and look at the girl. With intensity, threat. It was a look he saved for her when she was in trouble.

When they came out of the pet shop with the puppy in a carrier, her father looked left and right. Not at his daughter, shrinking into the dark space between two thrumming refrigerators.

Then the girl got into a taxi, and waved. And her father watched the taxi drive away as if it contained everything he owned.

二十九

KOJI STOOD IN front of the mirror and switched on the buzzing clippers. He watched the black hair peel from his scalp and fill the sink. Then he took a razor from the plastic wrapping and wet his head and removed the bristly stubble. And his eyebrows too, careful not to tug at the delicate skin. When he stepped back and observed himself naked, he found the rest of his body hair incongruous, dirty. He raised his arms and shaved his armpits. And then his genitals, lifting up his penis and stretching the translucent skin over his testicles, running the blade over the spidery veins.

He felt as if he'd been following her his whole life. Hard to consider what was existence before she stepped off the moon and sat down next to him.

What were dinosaurs?

What were continents floating on the Cambrian sea?

Once there was his grandmother. The group and his dying Leader. Then her.

But who was her father? Letting his daughter wander the streets at night. What if he hadn't been in Roppongi? He was surprised by the warmth of their blood, the look of disbelief on the man clutching his stomach.

Koji turned in the mirror. He liked his new form. Clean. Beyond human. Better.

He had one of her discarded PET bottles, plucked from a station trash can. Sometimes he put the neck to his mouth and closed his eyes. There were pictures of her jogging in the park, playing tennis.

Koji flushed his hair down the toilet. He showered and stepped from the cube of his tiny bathroom and switched out the light.

Then he opened his balcony and sat on the concrete floor, naked in the city.

三十

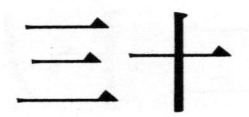

I WAS STANDING on the balcony of my university office. A canned coffee in one hand and stats on task accuracy in the other. Focus on neither. Beyond the jumble of rooftops and apartment blocks, the grey flotsam of suburbs and dormitory towns, the cone of Mount Fuji floated like a white temple on a blue sea.

I'd never climbed the volcanic summit. I tried, but the day I took a bus from Shinjuku, my brand new hiking boots ready for the three thousand metre ascent, thunder and lightning rippled about the mountain like warring gods. Rain hammered on the cafeteria roof at the base station, and as the bolts of electricity had hissed and crackled I'd thought about *Kaguya-hime*, how the Emperor had burned her potion of everlasting life when he realised he'd never see her again.

A month after saying goodbye to Kozue in Inakoshira Park, I could empathise. She'd seemingly vanished. Returned to the moon.

It wasn't long after the ride back to Tokyo, fiddling with the price tag on my backpack as the coach sluiced along the watery highway, that I caught the plane back to England. And started on the book, the grand distraction.

Or so I thought.

I went back inside and threw my canned coffee in the bin. When I grabbed my jacket from the chair and got ready to go home, my phone rang, buzzing on the table. It was Yuki, and I let it ring through to the voicemail.

She sounded older, wiser.

She said that Kozue wanted to meet me, and that she'd asked her to be my escort.

She said that we had to get a train out of Tokyo, and that if we didn't go this weekend we might not be able to go at all.

I looked at the papers on my desk, the books and journals documenting human behaviour. From the contested histories of Palaeolithic cave tribes to the evolution of the brain. Free will and hormones, nature versus nurture. Yet no trope on my personal folly. No theory to reference on what I should do and why.

**

Mazzy had been quiet, busy, I presumed, with school and friends. It was hard to define the atmosphere when I told her I was going away for Saturday night, and that I'd arranged for her to stay at Yamada's for the evening.

"Okay?"

She shrugged.

"I'll take that as a yes."

"Whatever."

"Michiko says she'll take you to the Ikegami sento, the one with black water."

"Cool."

She started bouncing the tennis ball she was holding, drumming it on the hardwood floor.

I said, "There are people downstairs."

"There are people everywhere."

She caught the ball and went into her room. I followed her as far as the hallway, and told her that we could take a trip to Fuji in a couple of weeks.

"It's covered in snow."

"And?"

"I know climbing season is finished because Larissa went with her mom on the last day you could go to the peak."

I talked about skiing in the Japanese Alps. "Near Nagano, on the Olympic slopes. You can bring Larissa."

"Maybe."

"Or Nikko. Where the monkeys bathe in volcanic pools."

I described how snowflakes settled on their heads like icy crowns, that group hierarchy could be observed by watching who groomed the alpha male, which apes had to wait in the frosty air.

"If I don't have too much school work."

"It's a plan."

I'd see tiny hand prints in the snow, trails where baby monkeys had walked through a pine forest.

**

On a sleek-nosed bullet train with armchair seats, we watched the city slide by on tinted glass. As if set designers had switched the urban scenery for snowcapped peaks and verdant rice fields.

With Yuki, I was going to Nikko. The hot spring town with a perfect lake and painted temples, a frozen waterfall.

Kozue.

I'd kissed Mazzy goodbye in the morning, and told her what time she was expected at Yamada's. She seemed nonchalant about my trip, and her maturity was as satisfying as it was distancing. In the rare moments I rationalised my actions, I knew, accepted, that I needed a woman, a lover, before my daughter left me for good.

And of course I was nervous. What was I really doing by getting on a train with a hostess tour guide? Who was I going to find? Part of the chase was the otherworldliness of the venture. The unexplained. In a world I watched and measured, the behaviour of my fellow human coolly observed, this was an enduring mystery.

Yuki was chatty on the ride north. She could talk about everything and nothing. From the comfort of the seats to the lunch in our bento boxes. I ordered a miniature bottle of white wine, not in celebration, just a drink to take the edge off the journey. I felt claustrophobic. Although I was escaping Tokyo, I was closing in on my narrow self.

Then we arrived in mountain air. Stepping from the train into an oxygen chamber. That deep and exaggerated inhale when you feel the sky in your lungs. A wide river sparkled, winter light skimming the shallow rapids. Black peaks and white snow, liquid sun on the rooftops.

"Is she going to meet us at the hotel?"

Yuki tucked her arm through my elbow as I wheeled her suitcase across the platform. "I have to call her later."

We walked up a small, main street, lined with souvenir shops and restaurants.

"*Tabun, ne.*"

Tabun. Maybe. Now I was sceptical. Maybe in Japanese usually meant no. Not a possibility. There was also the fear I was walking into a trap. A trap I'd constructed. What if she was still with the same man, married and content, and once again here was the *gaijin* intruder.

It was too early to check in to the hotel, and after dropping our luggage with the concierge we strolled around Nikko. We visited a giant, golden Buddha, and then walked beneath a lavishly decorated tori, where a four hundred year old carving of the three wise monkeys sat above the Toshu-go shrine.

I stood and stared at the famous apes. "Hear no evil, speak no evil."

"See no evil," completed Yuki.

It was the first time I'd heard her use English, and I realised there was more to her than I'd thought, that I'd underestimated her.

If the tourists looked away from the garish temples, they looked at us. The *gaijin* and his girl. Perhaps they were calculating the age gap. I tried not to catch our reflection, not wanting the contrast presented for my own eyes to judge.

After the stroll we checked into a large traditional ryokan, set within the hallowed temple grounds. Although plush, with deep carpets and uniformed staff at the ready, it was past its heyday. The receptionist copied down our names, either with utter disinterest or absolute professionalism, and we followed a kimono clad porter to an empty room. In the cupboard was a futon, two pillows, four white towels, a pair of yukatas and a kettle. Nothing else. I slipped off my shoes and walked across the tatami, sliding back the window and taking in the scent of pine.

Yuki inspected the bathroom, the complimentary biscuits by the kettle. Then she came up behind me and put her hand in my palm.

When I turned and let go she stepped back into the middle of the room. And without warning unzipped her skirt. She let it drop to the tatami, past a pair of hold up stockings and black pants. She stepped forward and nimbly slipped her fingers through my belt buckle. Her hands moved around my waist before the reflection of us in the window fixed my scruples. How vulnerable she looked. I backed away and told her to stop, that she didn't need to do anything she didn't want to because I was paying her.

"*Daijobu.*"

The screen door was open to a swathe of fir trees, green hills and blue sky.

"Let's go," I said, instructed. "See the waterfall, the frozen river."

Half naked, she stood in the milky light that reflected off the snowfields, and I bent down and picked up her skirt.

三十一

MAZZY TOOK OFF her jeans, picked them up, and folded them back into her closet. Then she grabbed a skirt from her drawer and pulled it on. She checked her hair in the mirror, applied another coat of lip gloss, and walked out of the apartment.

Fuck him.

She walked past the subway, the train she was supposed to be taking to Omori, where Yamada lived, and headed up towards Roppongi. Every shop window she walked past she saw her reflection. Older. Definitely older. And height with the heels. How they gave her hips curves that her Converse flattened out.

Larissa was waiting at the foot of Mori Tower, standing under the giant spider, waving. She wore leggings and dangly gold earrings, banned at school.

She said, "You look so hot."

Mazzy played down the compliment, as if she dressed like this everyday.

"What time shall we make the phone calls?"

"Let's get there first."

Larissa linked arms with Mazzy, and together they went down the escalators to the station. Both of them tested the allure of their outfits by smiling at the passing men. No mirror needed. The smiles came bouncing back. And bitchy stares too. Good. That meant she was someone worth looking at.

They took the train to Yokohama and walked around the quayside, riding the huge ferris wheel where Mazzy tried not to be shocked when Larissa told her she'd had sex with Legolas.

"I think he was a virgin." She was looking down at the water below their dangling capsule. "He said he'd done it before, but that was bullshit."

Then Larissa stared at Mazzy, and asked the question.
Mazzy lied, and said that of course she wasn't.

They ate tempura in a tenth floor restaurant that hovered over Chinatown. Larissa paid with her mother's credit card. Mazzy wanted to tell Larissa about her father and the girl in the taxi. But she wanted to forget it, too.

Then they headed to the Yokohama Blitz, a venue with no ID checks. Nothing. All Mazzy did was hand over the ticket that Larissa pulled from her purse.

"Where are we going to stay tonight?"

"Who fucking cares?"

They walked into the concert hall past rows of fans in band T-shirts, names and dates of gigs in different continents across their backs. There were a few foreign guys in the crowd, "English," Mazzy told Larissa. "Definitely."

Where the Englishmen leered, the Japanese men seemed fearful of the bold twosome levering their way towards the front, and parted for them to squeeze and shove through until they were wedged against the barrier.

"I'm so gonna crowdsurf," said Larissa, pulling a can of Red Bull from the waistband of her leggings. "Here."

Mazzy snapped it open and drank, passed it back.

Larissa let out a little scream. "Fuck, I could pee myself I'm so excited."

She watched Larissa drink and wished she had a sister.

"Shit, we better call."

"Now?"

"Before the gig starts."

Mazzy looked around the hall. It was filling up quickly. Fans in the rear seats unfurling banners and cheering, shouting out the names of songs and band members.

三十二

ON THE EDGE of a perfect lake, where stately clouds drifted over the grandeur of their own reflection and the granite brows of mountain peaks, Mazzy rang.

She said she was out with Larissa, and that it was too late to be heading over to Omori, and much easier to stay at her house. I stepped away from Yuki and stood by a cafe closed for the winter. And talked to my daughter. I explained that it was rude when Yamada was expecting her, and that she really should have told me sooner.

"Dad, it's so much easier to stay with Larissa."

She sounded stressed, amongst the Tokyo crowds.

"She's right here if you need to speak with her."

"If you say it's okay, it's okay."

"It is."

"Be good."

"Stop saying that."

Then she hung up. And I was left on the shore of a postcard, the blue sky bleeding into pink, where the sun went down like a light show arranged by the local tourist board.

Yuki was struggling on the ice, awkward in heeled shoes, and I put my arm around her as though she were kin, a daughter.

三十三

AND THEN THE band came out, swaggering, wired and glaring. The crowd roared and seethed. Mazzy felt the push of fans behind her, and Larissa gripped her arm and the two of them jumped and danced with the rest of the stadium. When the lead singer leapt down between the stage and the bouncers that separated him from the screaming fans, it was Mazzy and Larissa he came and sang for, of that they were certain.

"He so fucking sang to us," said Larissa. "Did you see him."

Mazzy was watching the band exit, how the bassist poured a whole bottle of water over his head.

"Come on," said Larissa, pulling at her wrist. "Let's get backstage."

At the rear of the venue they stood with a gaggle of Japanese fans, mostly women. The sharp wind cut through their jackets, cold clothes damp with sweat.

"If they come out and sign autographs, we've got to get an invite to the after party."

Larissa was standing at the doorway to the car park, where a tour bus with tinted windows idled.

"I got it," said Larissa. "Let's go flirt with the driver."

"You're doing the flirting."

Larissa took off her jacket and gave it to Mazzy. The driver was reading a manga comic, shoes off and socked feet crossed over the steering wheel. He saw them knock at the door, the cute half girl with braces and cleavage, the blonde girl with brown legs, probably American.

三十四

A DRAMATIC SCULPTURE in petrified glass, the frozen waterfall passed through an eyelet of rock and fell like a lace of ice into the deep gorge. Cold, I stood with Yuki on the observation deck. The wind bit sharply as the bright stars whirled above the peaks.

"*Samui.*" Yuki was shivering. She linked her arm around mine. "Let's go back to the hotel. Have a bath." She put her hand under my jacket. "Together, *ne*."

I stalled with the excuse of hunger, and we ate bowls of soba at a little shop on the road back to the hotel. Yuki slurped and twirled the noodles, skilfully wound down mouthfuls of buckwheat.

When she went to the bathroom I popped outside and rang Lenny, told him where I was and what I was doing.

"Props for tracking her down."

Then I explained Yuki, the deal. How I was paying her one hundred thousand yen to escort me to Kozue, and how that seemingly wasn't enough.

"She's persistent?"

"I make excuses."

"Maybe she likes you?"

"Help me out here."

Lenny went quiet. Beyond his breathing I could hear Tokyo, the beating city and its clamour.

"How old is she?"

I shrugged my shoulders. "Twenty something, I guess."

"Are you sure?"

Through the fogged windows of the noodle shop, I watched her walk back to the table.

"No," I said. "I'm not."

Lenny froze my blood. He told me that girls under eighteen would sleep with customers before the yakuza followed up with extortion deals and jail threats.

"Nothing's happened."

"Well keep it that way."

"Shit."

"They usually get proof, anyway."

I recalled her phone on the coffee table in the hotel, how it was rested on its side against the tea cup when she dropped her skirt.

"Sounds like a good ruse to me."

"I didn't do anything."

"Don't panic, man."

"Is she going to give me Kozue's address?"

"Did she give you her word?"

"She did."

Lenny guessed she would, and that Kozue probably made no difference to any plans they had for me, the *gaijin* who'd waltzed into The Island and bragged about his earning power.

"Fuck it. What a mess."

"Play it cool. Shit, the way Asian women are she might be thirty fucking five for all you know."

Yuki was looking at me through the window, waving. She wasn't thirty five. I thanked Lenny and hung up. Back in the shop she asked if I was okay, and I feigned the beginnings of a stomach problem, the excuse that would put me to bed early, alone.

三十五

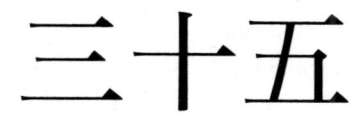

"NO WAY, GIRLS. Off the bus."

The road manager was English, a veteran of wayward bands and global tours. He took one look at the two of them sitting at the table, the flawless skin and train track braces, and then asked the Japanese driver why the fuck he was letting jail bait groupies on board.

Larissa played the interview card, the lie they'd hatched while waiting, how they needed to question the band for their college newspaper.

The manager laughed. "You are fucking kidding."

"It's a project."

"Let's go."

Larissa pleaded, smiled and pouted. Did the thing with her eyes that she practised in the mirror.

"Off."

He shooed them across the tarmac like scolded cats. As far as the gate that led from the stage door to the car park.

"Shit." Mazzy looked at Larissa, hoping for a plan. Something.

"Here they come."

The band came ambling towards the coach. Roadies carrying guitar cases, a security guard keeping the last of the groupies at arm's length. When Larissa saw two Japanese women climb up the coach steps and walk on board she shouted, "Fuck your music."

The lead singer turned around. "Don't hate me, gorgeous."

"Kiss me an apology."

"*Larissa*."

He was drunk and red faced, a towel dangling around his neck. He took one step off the bus before the road manager had a piece of his shirt and yanked him back as if he were a dog on a lead. "You get soup three times a day in Japanese nick."

"Bye bye, ladies." The singer drunkenly waved. "Come back next birthday." He blew a kiss as the door hissed shut.

Mazzy and Larissa watched the bus pull away, the wheeled party with their idols slipping into the Yokohama dark.

"Fuck."

Larissa took her jacket back from Mazzy and zipped it to her chin. The other women who'd been waiting had already left.

"Look how late it is." Mazzy held up her phone.

"So what?" said Larissa. "We'll stay in a love hotel."

"A love hotel."

"They don't have receptionists. You just walk in and pick a room from a vending machine."

"Have you stayed in one before?"

"Fucking manager," said Larissa. "What was his problem?"

Mazzy looked around the empty lot. There was a security guard closing a shuttered garage, locking doors for the night.

Beyond that was a park, a Japanese man sitting on a bench, alone.

三十六

KOJI WALKED BEHIND them into Yokohama. It was cold, and neither of them were wearing winter clothes. He was near enough to see that. When he got too close, and he could hear them talking and smell her perfume, he felt dizzy.

No stars but the neon glare.

No moon.

When they stopped at the Freshness Burger he walked straight past, crossed the road, and doubled back and stood in a phone box where he could see into the restaurant. They ordered and sat at a booth seat by the window. She had a chicken burger and a paper cup of Coke. She tied her hair back to eat, licked her fingers.

Koji saw it as one would a dream. Too fantastic.

And, predictably, the dream turned into nightmare when two American boys got out of a taxi and went inside and took the seat beside hers. The boy with a cap on back to front who said something and made her laugh. The dark haired one with sideburns shaved to a point and a single gold hoop earring.

He ripped off a chunk of doughnut and threw it at his friend. It bounced off his chest and landed on the table.

Mazzy laughed. They all did.

The taller one revealed a shaven head when he took off his cap. He slyly pulled a bottle of vodka from his jacket and handed it over to the friend who poured it into their drinks.

Larissa pouted and laughed with her wide mouth and bright braces.

Mazzy smiled at the man who looked like a pirate.

The one with the crew cut passed Larissa the bottle and she waited for the server to look away before she took a big gulp. Then she passed it to Mazzy who paused and looked again at the dark haired man who said something and shrugged his shoulders.

Then she drank. And then the boys drank, and the girls ate their food and laughed and Koji could see the decision that they'd leave the Freshness Burger together had already been made.

All the way to the door of the nightclub, Koji followed.

He saw the one with the earring put his hand on the small of Mazzy's back when they went down the steps through the entrance. He waited beside a bicycle parking rack. A police car drove past and he walked around the block and stood again in the same spot watching the queue descend towards the dull bass that pulsed from the basement.

After a while he went into a 7-11 and bought an energy drink. He drank it in one go and then walked back to the club. Before he crossed the road he took the knife from his jacket and palmed it into his sock. Then he went down the steps to the ticket kiosk. Two bouncers, one Japanese, and one a *gaijin* who patted him down, watched him through the doors into the bar area.

Koji stood in the humid dark. Silhouettes of dancers cut with lights.

He was hot in his jacket. Pushed and nudged by staggering drunks and flailing arms. Then he saw the boy with the cap, walking around the edge of the dance floor with two bottles of beer in each hand. The waiting girls at a table.

They toasted. They drank, luminous teeth in the ultraviolet. Purple skin and flashing laughter.

Koji sat on a low round stool. He watched the dancers, an army of step and sway. When the next song started there was a cheer, and Mazzy and Larissa and the two men leapt into the ring, perfectly in time with the automated routine. Everyone in the club knew the moves.

He wondered who would notice. If he walked into the centre of the dance floor and folded onto his own blade. The blood running out like a ribbon.

Then the song stopped and the girls linked arms and ran giggling to the ladies.

He bent down and pulled the knife from his sock. He thumbed it open and walked between the dancers. Towards the men. Staccato in the strobe. He was one step from their table, one act from the end, when a drunken student crashed into him and clutched at his shoulders for balance. Koji slung him to the floor, and was set upon by his friends.

三十七

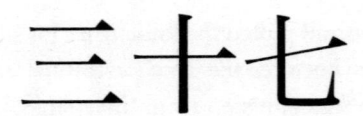

I WOKE IN the dead of night, soaked with sweat and tangled in the sheets. Yuki was curled on the other futon, fast asleep. I stood up and slid back the paper screen. A great, snow-muffled silence held the landscape, as if the mountains had been preserved in formaldehyde. I wanted to push open Mazzy's door, just to check she was safe. That she was okay. But I was in a rented room with a rented woman, company I was charged for by the hour. I picked up my phone and scrolled to her number. Then I thought about how angry she'd be if I woke her at this hour, cursing her nosey father.

I looked at Yuki, head on the pillow. Like a nun in prayer, palms pressed together under her chin.

No innocent dreamer. She was the elfin child from a fable of lies. The changeling nymph, beckoning the traveller through a darkened wood to the poisoned well.

I wanted the morning and its resolutions.

An end.

三十八

"I FEEL WEIRD."

Larissa was sitting on the toilet, Mazzy leant against the cubicle door.

"Do you have any water?"

"What?" Larissa unrolled the paper. "We lucked out meeting these guys."

"My hands are freezing. Feel." Mazzy held out her hands to Larissa.

"Why are your hands cold?"

"That's what I'm saying."

Larissa pulled up her leggings and stood. "Just dance some more."

They looked in the mirror. A Japanese girl came in and redrew her eyebrows with a pencil. Larissa opened her bag and brushed on another coat of lip gloss. She blew a kiss at Mazzy's reflection, and then vomited into the sink.

When they came out of the ladies room bouncers were throwing dancers to the floor. Glasses broke and tables turned. The kid with the cap was now hatless and bloody nosed, crawling between people's legs as if he were looking for a dropped key. The Japanese bouncer was trading punches with the earring pirate, the crack of bone on bone lost in decibels of music and screaming women. When the strobe light flickered it seemed like newsreel from the last century. In one frame the American was a champion pugilist, in the next he was gone, erased by the dark.

Mazzy grabbed Larissa and pulled her towards the exit, up the steps and back into the cold night.

三十九

EVERY FEW STEPS, Koji spat. Stringy globs of red. His tongue found the cut on the inside of his mouth, the tang of blood.

He looked left and right. The dark sea front. Landmark Tower like a pagan monolith. He guessed they would head into town, lights and people. He was walking and watching. He was sure the evening wasn't over, and when he saw them going down a ramp towards the reception of a love hotel he was certain he was blessed.

The room-vending machine was veiled by a curtain. He could hear them talking about paying and he heard the automatic entrance door click open and then click shut. He pulled back the curtain and noted the illuminated menu of available rooms. He pushed at the entrance door but it was heavy and made of steel. One room on the third floor was still lit. He waited. When the light switched out he walked back up the ramp and around to the rear of the hotel where he squatted between a dumpster and a minivan. He smelled petrol. Rotting food. He watched cockroaches skitter around his feet until he could bear it no more and climbed onto the dumpster and pulled himself up onto the first floor balcony. And then the second and the third.

四十

IN THE MORNING, when Yuki climbed into my futon and pressed her warm body against my back, I immediately got up and dressed. We went downstairs for breakfast in the hotel yukatas, my imaginary stomach bug miraculously improved. The dining area looked onto emerald pine, the frost on the leaves like a dust of icing. Starched white tablecloths blazed with sunlight, and each place was set with a multitude of breakfast paraphernalia. We took our seats and elderly women in kimonos ferried us trays of steaming bowls. Rice and miso soup. Grilled fish and seaweed. A raw egg. Pickles and pulses. I wasn't particularly hungry, but it seemed of the utmost importance that I finished my food. That I could earn the right to demand an address, Kozue.

On the next table was a foreigner. Scandinavian. Maybe Norwegian. In stilted Japanese he told his partner, a woman twenty years younger than his greying sixty, to order more tea. She dutifully did, calling over the scurrying waitress.

We caught eyes, once. He looked at Yuki, and then at me. Smirking, as if together we shared some victory of age over youth.

Yuki poured my tea, and I noticed she'd taken out her contacts. For the first time I saw the true colour of her iris, a pale, sandy brown. Much lighter than most Japanese.

I reached across and took the pot from her hand, and poured out her cup. She said thank you, and drank with her head down.

She seemed deflated, lost. I'd done nothing untoward. But after breakfast, when I walked out of the hotel room with Kozue's address scrawled on a menu, I felt like I'd stolen something.

**

Finally, I was going to see Kozue.

I walked from the lobby into the thin, mountain air. In the car park men shovelled grit onto frozen puddles. Water dripped from the eaves of the hotel roof, and a thread of smoke unravelled from the chimney. I felt for the address in my coat pocket and scanned the map the concierge had drawn. Following his pencilled trail, I crunched along gravel paths that cut between the painted shrines. There was snow on the temple steps, a barefoot monk in a cotton robe. Icicles hung like spikes of glass waiting to impale the tourists who clapped their hands and offered prayers, dropping coins through wooden grates and taking photos of the gods carved into the elaborate columns.

It was very quiet beyond the sightseeing spots, and Nikko was any other rural, shrinking town. A decrepit shopping parade, abandoned restaurants, and shuttered souvenir shops stocked with faded postcards and decorative fans. I passed a ghost hotel with cracked window panes, the Vacancy sign an invite for haunting. Across Japan the negative birthrate was steadily decimating populations of their youth, and fittingly, the only other pedestrian was an ancient woman bent in half by her folded back, shuffling along with a bag of vegetables swinging awkwardly against her leg.

By the petrol station, where the concierge had instructed me to cross the road, a uniformed attendant stood rigidly hoping for traffic. Out of courtesy to his patience I waited for a green signal. I turned into a quiet neighbourhood of traditional family houses with large, neat gardens, thriving with well kept plants and manicured trees, a bounty of glowing tangerines.

My nervous, fraught energy, trembling into optimism.

But when I found that the address was a shop selling pottery, I guessed I'd been played.

Again.

I walked up the path and slid back the wooden door, tinkling a small bell. The display area was unstaffed. Shelves of teapots, cups and plates lined the walls.

"*Gaijin.*"

A small boy stood in the doorway to the workshop. He wore a heavy knit sweater and blue dungarees covered in clay. Beyond the shock of his black hair I could see a potter's wheel, rows of plates waiting to be fired.

"*Konnichiwa.*"

"*Mama.*"

I heard a chair pushed across a stone floor, footsteps. A woman. "I'll be through in a moment."

I reached over to a shelf and picked up a sake jug. When I felt the sloping contours, I knew that it was hers.

She appeared in the doorway, a passing glance before she returned to wiping her hands clean with a towel.

Before she realised who'd walked into her shop.

"Ben."

I sat in a small conservatory at the back of the house, overlooking a lively stream twinkling with sunlight. There was a roughly hewn easel in the corner, the worn frame splashed with fading colours. Kozue carried in an electric bar heater and turned it towards where I sat on a wooden chair.

"I knew you'd walk in here one day."

She went out to fetch us coffee and her son came into the room with a toy truck and an ambulance. He gave me the ambulance, and when Kozue came back in I was on the floor pushing it along an imaginary highway.

"Akira likes you." She put the drinks down on a trestle. "He's usually shy." She brushed the hair from his face.

I got off my knees and sat down on the chair. And apologised.

"For what?"

"I shouldn't have come here."

She picked up a spoon and dug into the sugar. "Two?"

"You remember?"

"I'm surprised you have any teeth left." She stirred the coffee and passed over the mug. "How did you find me?"

I explained the club, the contact information I got from Yuki. I didn't add that she was waiting in a hotel around the corner.

Kozue shook her head. "No one ever leaves."

I sipped the coffee, said thank you. She'd barely aged. Fine lines around her eyes. Wrinkles from smiling. A calmness to her manner, no longer the restless woman.

I was about to apologise, again, for connecting her to a past she'd tried to forget.

"I remember everything," she said. "That moment in the bar, walking onto the street because I knew you'd follow me. Every single detail."

I didn't need to ask if Akira was her son, but I did want to know about his father.

"He's a good man. From Okinawa."

"And he'd be okay with me sitting in your house?"

She shrugged. "He's in a quarry buying clay. He won't be back for hours. All we're doing is having coffee, right?"

I nodded, drank. I looked at the bare walls of her workshop, and asked if she still painted.

"I stopped."

"And started sculpting?"

Akira climbed onto her knee, nuzzling under her arms.

"I'd still be hostessing if I hadn't created a name worth collecting."

"I searched for you and nothing came up."

"I invented a person. A new self. A new name. The space I created from was true, otherwise the art wouldn't have meant anything."

She smoothed Akira's fringe, stroking her son like a cat. She explained how she'd bought her way out of the yakuza, her father's debts, by selling paintings.

"I used to draw faces when I was girl. Detailed portraits. Then I started hostessing, and the portraits reflected what I thought of people. That essence became something darker. I was drawing faces, but with monsters behind the masks."

Akira repeated the word monster. She kissed his head, told him he was a good boy.

"Strangely enough, the art world wasn't so different from hostessing. I could work a room and name my price at a gallery launch."

I looked out of the window, through the wooden frame of the empty easel. The sun was setting behind jagged peaks, as if shapes cut from black paper.

"I shouldn't be here."

"You are. And you were. You got into a car with no idea of where you were going and ended up in my apartment."

Her room above Hiroshima. The clouds above the city like smoke from a fire.

"When I stood on your balcony and saw you putting on make up, I knew the paintings were yours."

I told her I was sure I'd seen figures that weren't there when I woke up.

Kozue laughed. "You weren't imagining them. I brushed them out. I turned them into trees and rocks."

Akira had fallen asleep in her arms, head flopped across her lap. Kozue lifted up her son and laid him on the sofa. She asked about Mazzy, my life. She sat forward, closer. The zoom lens of her gaze. The lustrous hair. I felt free, a naked being. I confessed that I loved my daughter, too much. And that given the chance I'd have loved her.

"Too much."

"Don't say that."

"It's true."

"We had something," Kozue said. "Sudden and strange. The world was dead. I was painting dead people. Then you arrived. Like a man fallen out of the sky."

"It was a curious thing."

"Like a folk story."

"That needed a happily ever after?"

Kozue turned to her napping son, his arm thrown out over the sofa, the toy truck in his tiny fist.

"Kozue."

She reached across and clutched my hand, linked her fingers between mine. And kissed me.

A goodbye.

I left her at the door of her little shop, with her pots and cups, the lumps of clay ready to take on new forms.

四十一

THE BRIGHT SUN hurt his eyes. Koji returned to his apartment where construction workers in yellow hats milled around the foyer. An engineer with a clipboard asked why he hadn't yet left the building. Koji looked at his name tag. The company badge. He kept his hands in his pockets and walked into the lift as the engineer threatened to call the police if he was still there tomorrow.

He unlocked his door and closed and bolted it behind him. His tiny apartment. A room that would be gone in two days time. Dust and memory. His memory. Because who else would look at this point of sky and know that a man once lived and breathed right here above the city.

Koji thought about this. Then he went into his bathroom and switched on the light. Smears of dried blood on his cheek, the backs of his hands. He leant against the sink and stared at himself for a long time, as if his reflection might do something of its own accord. He stared until he wasn't sure which way he was facing. Whether he was looking in or out at himself.

He only moved when he noticed a thread of gold caught on his sleeve, a strand of blonde hair.

四十二

ON THE TRAIN back from Nikko, Yuki hooked her arm around my elbow, and put her head on my shoulder, and slept. She felt as light as a bird. I watched the landscape flicker by like filmstrip, mountains levelling out to fields and towns, bright green paddies and concrete shopping centres. I closed my eyes. There was a dream about Mazzy, the recurring one, how she smiles and waves, and then runs up the beach towards the sea.

I rang and sent her a text, but got her voice mail.

I woke up in Tokyo station, slumped against the train window, my folded jacket a makeshift pillow. Yuki had gone, and after looking over the headrest I realised the entire carriage had disembarked, leaving me the last person onboard. I couldn't see Yuki on the platform, or anybody else for that matter. I presumed she was in the lavatory. Or, out of some protracted Japanese formality, had left me to sleep.

Still, it was very quiet.

I put on my jacket and looked along the aisle, and then through the doors into the next carriage. Not a soul. I looked again at the empty platform and wondered if I'd dozed while we'd pulled into a maintenance depot.

Then I stepped off the train. Volts of fear. No guards or passengers. Silence. I walked, and then jogged down the escalators to the ticket gates.

The waiting hall was empty. When I tried to exit, the automatic barriers snapped shut.

"*Sumimasen*," I shouted. "*Sumimasen*."

No answer.

I pushed through the barriers and stood before the news kiosk, scanning for signs of life. Today's papers. Rows of fresh cream cakes lined the patisserie stalls. Had I missed an evacuation call? Was I about to be engulfed by a tsunami or melt in a radiation cloud?

I heard a high pitched voice from the basement aisle of shops and restaurants and stomped down the escalators.

The noise was a giant teddy bear, bleating a recorded sales mantra. It should have been a packed walkway.

I sprinted along a corridor to the Maronuchi Exit. Emerging into another empty ticket hall, I again shouted, "*Sumimasen.*" Nothing. I dashed over to the information counter and checked the office. More unmanned booths. Open tills showing thousands of yen.

I was sure I'd missed news of an emergency, and was furious that no one had nudged me awake.

And where the hell was Yuki?

I ran up two flights of stairs, past the deserted police box, and out into the middle of the square. Just the looming towers of glass. No cars or buses.

"Hello?"

No one.

"*Hello?*"

The road should be clogged with traffic. Taxi ranks lined with cars. Perhaps a bomb was about to blow up Tokyo Station. A North Korean warhead was homing in to obliterate a city that had been cleared while I napped on the bullet train.

If the buildings were about to come tumbling down, I needed to be away from steel and glass, and ran towards the open space of the Imperial Palace. When I saw my running figure reflected in the curved windows of the Shin-Marunochi building, it was the first dreadful confirmation that I wasn't dreaming. That and the cartilage clicking in my knee. I ran along the central reservation between rows of flowerbeds, across the junction and over the moat into the palace grounds.

Out of breath, I slowed and turned back to the station. A silent construction site. Stalled cranes and empty sky, the cold wind. The only movement the scurrying, dry leaves, rasping along the pavement.

I pulled out my phone and rang Mazzy. Again, her answer phone.

I jogged, and then I ran, between small pines that dotted the lawn, heading into the setting sun. With the wind at my back, and the dead leaves streaming ahead, it seemed we were being sucked into a dying star. Passing the litter of a homeless camp, beer cans and a flu mask, empty cigarette packets and a water bottle, rubbish had never been so comforting. This was the most human thing I'd seen.

Beyond the trees I could see the palace, the gracefully curved roof, the moat and the stone wall, vacant sentry boxes. I could walk up to the house of the most precious and protected family in Japan. Stroll through the front door and nose around in the Emperor's bedroom.

I didn't care. I needed to know where Mazzy was. I ran along the empty highway, my knee shooting pain. After failing to break the lock on a bike I fell into a panicked walk, occasionally jogging, always looking to see if anyone else was around.

I ran down the middle of the road. My wooden soles slapped loudly, echoing between shop windows and company lobbies. The only other sound was my laboured breathing, until I reached Shiba Park at the foot of Tokyo Tower. Then crows, cawing from a ginkgo tree as I hurried to my apartment.

I didn't trust the lift and skipped up ten flights of stairs, rattling every letterbox in case other residents had missed the evacuation. How I preferred that reasoning to a void. That would mean people gathered in shelters, a hubbub of voices.

Not the silence when I opened my door.

Crushed. I ran from room to room. I went onto my balcony and surveyed the rooftops, the redundant buildings. I bellowed and screamed myself hoarse. I had conversations with the vacuum, begging the hidden to show themselves. Tokyo was an empty set, the actors backstage and the audience gone home.

I called for my daughter, shouting her name across the streets. No answer.

Nothing.

I'd left Nikko on a busy train and arrived in a hollow city.

I splashed my face with water, checked my reflection in the mirror. That it was still me. I slapped my cheeks until they burned and the blood was pounding through my inner ear. I clenched my fist and punched myself, knuckles against skull, rapping on the brain.

No world returned with a throbbing temple.

I scrawled a note and stuck it to Mazzy's bedroom door, promising I'd be back by dark.

Then I went downstairs, kicked my bike from the stand, and pedalled onto the main road. I had one look in the police box, and then rode up the shopping parade, past the tea shop and the French bakery, towards the bright steel of Mori Tower.

At the plaza an automated voice warned me to take care. A voice. A woman. Telling me to be careful on the escalators.

I felt stupid. Scared and baffled.

The silver steps revolved and I carried on my bike. At the top of the escalator was the faux German market. Snapped-together shacks in mock pine selling mulled wine and schnitzel. It should be teeming with shoppers. I wheeled my bike into the tower lobby, kicked out the stand, and walked through gates usually guarded by men in white gloves and peaked caps. I flicked glances over my shoulder, trying to catch out the phantom stalker, a following presence I felt despite the utter desolation.

All the lifts were waiting. I hit the button for the top floor, hoping the doors would open to a smiling receptionist, a polite bow and a lipstick smile.

No one.

The empty lighthouse at the top of the world, surrounded by stellar blue. I looked through the windows at the map of a city, the lifeless metropolis. I walked the observation deck and searched a dead panorama. For one vertiginous second I thought about throwing myself through the glass, falling with the shards and smacking the concrete.

But what would happen to Mazzy?

Then a lone crow glided from a street light and perched on an advertising hoarding, scraping its talons on the metal frame. When the crow upped and flew towards Shibuya, I took a lift back down to the lobby, got on my bike and followed.

I could hear my breathing, ticking wheels and the chain along the cogs. I knew that subjects in isolation experienced auditory hallucinations, that voices could be generated by loneliness. As sure as I could hear my own, plaintive call from the highway. Singing out to the empty streets like a forlorn rag and bone man.

Riding into Shibuya, a minuscule figure beneath the looming towers, I wondered if I was dead. A netherworld powered by the last sparks of my consciousness. No Pearly Gates. No reincarnation. Just a cold, glittering city. The sole occupant.

I rode through the main concourse of the train station, under a roof that should be vibrating with carriages. I pedalled past a flower stand selling bunches of roses, freshly picked and immortal with colour. I cycled under the bridge towards the bronze Hachiko statue, the sculpture of a dog that waited for the owner who never returned.

Mounted on every building around the intersection were the giant LED screens. Switched off. The white dots shrunk into black space.

In the middle of the crossing I put my bike on the stand and sat down. I should be trampled by the crowds, a rush of motorbikes and taxis. Instead I waited. Like a bronze dog. I looked into the cafe where I'd taken Mazzy on her first day here. If I focused hard enough could I jump back into that moment?

Any moment.

I got on my bike and pedalled past shops and restaurants, along the avenue of crimson maple trees. How appropriate that the roof of the National Stadium looked like a capsized ship.

Then again the crow. Flying towards Meiji Shrine. I followed, pedalling along a path speckled with ginkgo leaves and pine needles. Yoyogi Park should be filled with kids rehearsing plays.

Girls in maid outfits wailing with an out of tune guitar. The Elvis dancers, twisting and turning in their ripped leather jackets and gelled back hair.

I rode under the torii that marks the shrine entrance. The bike rattled across the gravel, tinkling the bell as I bounced a track through the small copse surrounding the sacred grounds.

More crows flew towards Shinjuku, like smoke might draw from an open window. Beyond the forest I could see a flock gathering above the Hotel Centurion.

Where I'd spent my last night with Kozue.

Through the empty streets I followed their flapping wings. At the foyer I carried my bike up the steps and dropped it clattering to the lobby floor. Then I jumped into the lift. I had to see the room, the bed. To know that she wasn't there. That we both weren't. The feeling that I'd find another version of myself was growing by the second, and I ran along the corridor.

The door was ajar, and slowly, I walked in. My trousers and shirt on the carpet. Clothes I no longer possessed. The bathroom was shut, and I knocked.

"Who is it?"

The muffled voice was mine. I tried the handle but it was locked, so I stood back and kicked off the bolt.

Water sloshing back and forth. Wet footprints. Her make up on the sink. Black eye-liner and lipstick. A space on the steamed mirror wiped clear.

I stumbled out of the bathroom. Crows swirled around the hotel like sheaves of burnt paper, and I reached up and opened the window. I was standing on the ledge when I saw the plane. A jet liner, high and bright. I shouted and waved, calling down the search team. When the plane looped in a slow, silent curve, I saw it was made of paper.

Yamada's design. The pretty white glider banked through wide turns, never losing height. When we'd followed its flight on the park, we were the protectors. Now the plane was my guardian.

I descended to the lobby and ran outside. The crows had gone, but the plane was still sailing the breeze, looping back and forth over Kinokuniya. The bookshop. If I could hold a copy of my book, read my name on the jacket, then I'd know that I once existed. With others. *Groups, Gangs and Belonging* could hardly be written in a peopleless city.

I sprinted across the footbridge and banged open the doors. Aisles of best-selling novels and international newspapers. Gaudy magazines filled with celebrities and film stars.

In the popular science section I scanned the spines. My trembling finger noted that the authors beginning with M didn't include Monroe.

Then I saw the cover. What at first looks like a strutting gang is on closer inspection a group of disparate individuals: a policeman next to a football hooligan, a schoolgirl, a businessman, a punk, an old woman with a cane, a soldier and an anti-war protester.

But the name wasn't mine.

In block capitals, where Ben Monroe should have been printed, it read Per Lindstrand. Lydia's new partner.

Mazzy's new father.

I dropped the book and fled down the escalators, crashing through a fire exit onto the walkway above Shinjuku station. I collapsed. I pulled at my hair and pressed my palms against my eye sockets, as if I could force the correct vision onto my brain.

Then I heard the slow hiss of water, pebbles jumbling in a broken wave. I was sitting on a beach in California. Sunlight danced on the sea. Lifeguards chatted, patrolled the shoreline. I stood up and trudged across the sand, ducking under umbrellas, stepping around towels and glistening bodies. I could smell coconut sunscreen. I bent down and scooped up a handful of hot sand.

I caught sight of the red and white golf umbrella we always used as shade, and I walked across the beach until I was right behind the parasol.

"Look, daddy."

Mazzy.
Gone.
With the sea and its breaking waves.
My baby daughter.

Back in Tokyo, the empty city. A burst of sun between the buildings. Light on the train tracks. A train on the light tracks.

A train.

Without passengers. The carriages rattled across sleepers, and the lone service shuttled into Shinjuku station. I ran down the staircase, jumped the ticket barrier and sprinted along the concourse, terrified the train would leave without me. The jingle played to warn that the doors were closing and I dived inside.

As the train pulled away, I realised that I wasn't the only passenger. In the next carriage, looking over her shoulder and walking away, was Mazzy. I yanked open the door and leapt across the couplings, hurrying along the aisle to keep her in sight.

The train was gathering speed, shooting through stations, accelerating until the lights were neon smears. We span through revolutions of Tokyo, faster and faster, beyond the screeching metal and rattling tracks until I was weightless, adrift in the calm of zero gravity.

Swimming with Mazzy in a Greek cove, floating in sunlight.

Bang.

Crumpled on the carriage floor. The train stopped. Shadows on the platform. Figures. Tall, and imposing.

Crows.

Huge, imperious crows. They cocked their heads and studied me. A specimen. One of the crows let out a low cackle, and the other birds cawed in reply. My body was meat, prone before the gleaming beak that jutted into the carriage. I pushed myself away from the snapping jaw. The flock rustled their wings and passed a length of steel from beak to beak. When the head crow bent the rod into a hook, I knew it was the tool to pull my body from the train. I jumped up to run, but the crow snagged my coat and dragged me to the door. Kicking and screaming, I was hauled onto the platform and plucked into the air.

Dangled above the city, like a mouse in the grip of a falcon. Helpless. Yet secure in the talons that I was something not to be dropped.

There was peace to be held like prey. To be carried.

We rose above chequered rice fields, the concrete towns and metallic cities. The crow rode higher on heated thermals, and the landscape faded, vanished into sky.

**

I looked down onto broken, sunlit clouds. They flecked the ocean like a great blue blanket pocked with feathers.

I was staring from a plane window. Not hung in the grip of a giant crow, dangled above a void.

A smiling flight attendant asked if I wanted chicken or fish.

"Chicken, please."

I peeled back the foil cover and ate. The clarity of each forkful. Meat to mouth. Chew. It was blissfully terrible. Real. The teriyaki sauce tasted like it had been painted on with a brush used to creosote a garden fence.

I said, "My father used to creosote the fence."

The woman sitting beside me said, "Ben."

"At the end of summer."

"Do you want tea, Ben?"

"He used to let me prise the lid off the tin."

The woman beside me took the tea from the flight attendant. She put the cup on my plastic tray. I ripped open a pack of sugar and poured, watching the granules melt into liquid. Then I asked the woman next to me if I could have her sugar because I knew she drank her tea without a sweetener.

She put her hand on my forearm. She was crying. It seemed perfectly ordinary that she was sat in the seat next to me. Lydia. I had two sugars, and she had none.

四十三

SHE SAID UFOS would come from the sky and rescue him. There would be ships of light riding down the stars.

She promised.

The planet of eternal life.

Koji sat on his apartment roof for two nights. Sleeping in the day and waking at dusk to follow the few suns bright enough to outshine the Tokyo glare. When he was a boy he watched lumps of ferric rock streak above the rice paddies. And his grandmother would tell him the story of *Kaguya-hime*. The moon princess. The beauty too precious for earth.

He watched the blue sky flood the dark.

How the moon sank like a white stone.

He felt the city wake on his skin. Rumblings of the first trains, the empty carriages. Then the carriages filling, crowding. All those bodies pressed into a single mass. He pictured the silent commuters moving without the train. A rectangular puzzle of heads and limbs hovered above the tracks.

Her breath on his palm.

The soft blonde hair.

He watched the crows, gliding, swirling the thermals on a wing beat. He saw the purple flash of their shiny feathers.

If he died here they might take his body into the sky.

But there was no time for that, and the crows spiralled down to alight in the bare branches of the cherry trees in the car park.

While he was hiding on the rooftop, a demolition team had bored holes into the concrete pillars of the foundations. Men carrying reams of cables and detonators. Priming the lower floors with explosives.

All morning he listened to the engineers talk to each other through megaphones. Echoes counting minutes, seconds.

Then it went very quiet, and he heard a siren.

Crows took flight from the trees, and although Koji was lying on hard concrete, when the building dropped away it seemed as if the whole world was falling, and it was he who was rising.

跋

WE TREK THE bare hills behind San Diego, following signposted trails across broken mantle, paths along creeks that chatter with streams. We head out at dusk, when the sun has abated and the air has cooled to a pleasant walking climate.

Lydia still had my old hiking boots in a box at the back of her garage. It was the first thing we did, hike a rocky peak. After she walked me off a plane from Japan, hand on my elbow, guiding me through Los Angeles airport like the fragile infirm I was.

I am.

Driving along the Pacific Highway.

Reassembling the world.

The fragments.

My ex-wife at the wheel, that savage beauty in her windblown hair, talking.

Explaining.

How she'd packed her bag within minutes of receiving the call from Japan. That a man from the US consulate had met her at Narita airport and told her what she already knew about Mazzy. About me. She'd followed the man through an express customs channel, past the barriers, to where drivers held up name cards and parents hugged their returning children.

From the back seat of a car she watched the scenery emerge, and then fade. Thickets of bamboo. Retail outlets and factories. Hard to see what was outside the window when all she could think of was Mazzy.

This much I know.

That Yamada had called me when I was on the way back from Nikko. News about a body in the woods at the foot of Mount Fuji. A blonde girl. Slight and pretty. I answered the phone, I'm told. Spoke with him and confirmed that I understood. That Mazzy was missing. An hour later I got off the train, I presume, and erased my identity, a capital city of its population.

My daughter.

Later that afternoon Yamada picked me up from Ikebukuro station. Alone. A train guard pulled me off a carriage after passengers reported a man sitting on the floor and screaming. They dragged me into an office, took my phone and rang Yamada, the last name in my call history. I spoke to him, he said, with a clinical detachment. He said I was organised and calm. Practical. That I communicated with people at the embassy and the police station.

I have no memory of this, just his word.

He said I was compos mentis when we stood in a sterile morgue lit by sodium bulbs. That I spoke with Larissa's father, and from a photo posted on his daughter's Facebook page of a themed Hello Kitty room in a love hotel, we'd deduced where our children were and sent in the police to kick down a door.

The body on the table in the morgue, pale under the strip lighting, was a Lithuanian girl who worked in a hostess bar.

Larissa was found on the bed, and Mazzy on the bathroom floor. The MDMA in their bloodstream was tainted with baking soda. The door was locked from the inside, yet both the girls had been arranged into the recovery position. This, the police couldn't explain.

But it had saved their lives.

Not until I was zipping along the highway to San Diego, all that sky and sea on the windscreen, the tears streaming down Lydia's cheeks, did I fully comprehend where I was.

Who and when.

That the hand in mine was Mazzy's.

I told Lydia to pull over. I opened the door and jumped out. Father and daughter stood and hugged on the edge of the road, buffeted by the wind of passing cars. Over and over she said she was sorry and I cradled her head and apologised and held her tight as the trucks hammered along the interstate.

That I could have lived my life without this feeling. To hold Mazzy this close. My precious baby. The little girl I carried and fed. The toddler on my shoulders who marched me around the garden and sang nursery rhymes and laughed and cried and slept in my arms.

I am the man she has brought back from the void.

The father resurrected by his daughter.

**

Lydia has arranged for me to stay with her colleague, Dr Gayle, a combat veteran with electric blue eyes and silver hair. A man with a single ear and a burn scar melting down his neck. He told me to call him Gayle. I have a room in his converted barn, the kind of building you might still see on the edge of a prairie, hay piled in the loft like gold.

Rather than sitting on the psychiatrist's couch, I'm clearing a fire break for his insurance company, trimming back the scree.

"Grounding," he calls the therapy. "A smart cut on your hand sure proves the now."

He has thick, calloused palms, and together we chop wood on the hillside. For the last week I've woken at sunrise and swung an axe. When Gayle rests from chopping wood he swigs water from a bottle clipped to his belt. On the first day I asked if his canteen was US army issue and he laughed and told me it was on sale at Walmart.

He also told me about Agatha Christie. How she vanished from her house for eleven days before turning up in a hotel with no recollection of where she'd been.

"She'd suffered a fugue."

"And she was fine?"

"In perfect physical health. Yet a week and a half was missing from her mind."

Gayle counsels soldiers with post traumatic stress disorder. Teenage boys who picked their flung limbs from tree branches.

Men who battle in dreams of war that appear more real than the bed they wake.

"The kids come back from service, a brotherhood of fear and violence in deserts and mountains, squalid mud towns with mines in the alleyways, and then sit alone in a room."

We work in the mornings and talk in the afternoons. Occasionally he'll stop and rest, lean on the axe handle and speak.

"You thought she was gone."

He asks me to question him. Not to eschew his prognosis with silence.

"That you'd lost her."

From the moment on the train, when Yamada had rung me about a body, my missing daughter, I'd invented a new reality.

"Your brain redesigned perception. You functioned. Walked and talked. But reprogrammed the world."

Gayle talks about a college student in New York. A girl in a sports bra and running shorts, presumed kidnapped or murdered, who turned up swimming in the Hudson. Three weeks of her life absent, gone. There was video footage of her buying food in a convenience store, talking with the clerk.

"Total amnesia."

"But I have a memory."

Gayle unscrews his canteen and passes it over. He watches me drink, chewing on a blade of grass like a farmhand.

"I interviewed a vet who'd been a truck driver in Baghdad. Lost a friend in an ambush on his convoy. Carried the guilt from that day on because he didn't get out of his rig and fire the Glock he had in his glove box. Last year he sets out for DC to visit a dying friend. Four days later he wakes up in the back of his car. In Denver. Dehydrated and scared. Convinced he'd just been driving around a desert in Iraq, lost in a sandstorm."

I pass Gayle the water and wipe my forehead.

"Do I know what was real?"

"Maybe you ran. Maybe you sat gibbering on a park bench."

"Yamada said my bike was missing."

"And you left the note on Mazzy's door."

I'd been back to my apartment. This was a fact. That I'd walked into an empty room. And if I did scan the rooftops, the teeming streets, I'd ignored the crowds and constructed a city absent of others, my daughter included, because I didn't have the power to lose her.

"Again."

"A fugue in defence."

We cut more wood.

"Armour."

**

We clear a ring of scrub around the barn, tramping noisily to shoo away the rattlers. Gayle works in total focus, as if each saw stroke or axe fall were his last. Sweating, but clear-headed, I tell him that I feel good. Centred is the word I use. Whatever I mean by this. He says that a bushfire in the next valley would burn down his house.

After the labour we sit on the porch and drink iced tea. And talk some more. He tells me what Yamada told him, that even when Mazzy had been let out of hospital, I was walking a vacuum.

"You sat with her, but didn't accept she was there."

We got to the love hotel minutes after the police had smashed down the door. I rode with Mazzy in the ambulance, held her hand. I'm told.

"Nothing came up on your MRI scan." Gayle scans the neurologist's report, the graphs and charts. "No lesions or brain damage."

I pour him another iced tea.

"But this is normal for psychogenic amnesia."

"It felt as real as this." I gesture at the sky, cars glinting on the highway. "The clink of ice cubes in your drink."

He looks at the landscape. Californian born, eyes the colour of the sea. Fancifully, I picture his grandfather swinging a pick, panning a muddy river.

"It is unusual," he admits. "The clarity of recall."

Gayle asks me about the days leading up to Nikko. He explains that fugue states are often primed by the reappearance of persons or events from a past trauma, and I tell him everything. What I can. About Kozue. The hitch-hike and the affair. He makes notes as I talk, his pencil scratching away.

"You have any photos?"

"Of Kozue?"

"Kozue."

I don't. He makes more notes, and I tell him to stop writing. I go into the barn and open my suitcase. I take out the bundle of paper and carry it onto the deck.

"She made this."

He unwraps the gift. Carefully. The cup looks very delicate in his cracked palms, the black lacquer finish, the gold leaf pattern. "It's exquisite." He turns it once, and then passes it back.

Kozue had fetched the cup down from a shelf in her studio and wrapped it in rice paper. She made me promise to never let anyone else drink from it.

"You think I invented this woman?"

He shakes his head. I hold the cup in two hands. I can feel the weight of her touch in the rim. Her fingers shaping the circle. I pour some iced tea from my glass into the cup, and drink, before wrapping it back into the paper.

Gayle studies my every move, and I tell him I had to know what happened to her.

"That I hadn't fucked that up too."

He says I'm wrong.

"What time's your daughter coming over?"

**

Mazzy eats with me at night. She bought me a new pair of hiking boots a few days ago, knocking on the kitchen window.

Mazzy.

"It'll be dark in an hour."

It seemed remarkable.

"You still want to go."

Standing there with the dangling boots.

"Mom said we have to take a stick, in case of mountain lions."

Lydia drives her up around sunset. Sometimes we chat with Gayle. The four of us talking it out. Sympathy and anger. Not blame. I hold Lydia in high reverence, not that I ever didn't, for listening to my vain pursuit of Kozue, the woman I'd found, and lost, when I was missing her.

And my precious Mazzy. Patient with her dysfunctional parents. Her father. Then talking about her anger, the emotion flowing from her like an exorcism. How she followed me from the apartment into Roppongi, and then saw me chasing Yuki up the street in Shibuya.

I explained, I think. And she understood.

I hope.

Gayle controls the three of us like a conductor. He understands, and skilfully ignores, my awarenesses of his methods. He contends that I sought out Kozue because the daughter was beyond her father. Because I was alone. That the Yokohama gig and the ecstasy was Mazzy's way of punishing me, and perhaps herself, for not showing affection, love.

Although I know the limits of counselling, the coffee table chat with strategic words, the meetings are medicine. Therapy. We've sat and defined the fact and fiction of our family dynamics, the denial and delusion. Moreover, the discussions have realigned and confirmed my own consciousness. Not a Descartes self-hood of knowledge and understanding, but an awareness of identity from sensation and perception. The startling now. My beloved daughter, right there.

After we talk and hike, we eat. I chop and wash vegetables, prepare salads. Pleasure in arranging food on the plate. Juice bursting from a ripe tomato. Touchable, visceral life. I went fishing with Lydia's brother at the weekend. In the surf on the edge of the booming Pacific. I watched the breaking waves, how the water folds and shatters, rebuilds.

Sometimes I think of Tokyo, gathering fragments, clips of reality hidden within the fugue. Sitting in the car with Yamada and watching a stop light change to green. Signing a form in the police station. Another father in another country. What poor man got news of his baby girl.

I'm afraid of falling into myself, of losing it all, that I might wake up in an empty city. So I talk to Gayle or drive into town. I walk the domed shopping malls and buy peppers and aubergines. Aspire to an ordinary man doing the groceries. I drink coffee and eat doughnuts, pick up magazines and read the gossip columns.

It wasn't until yesterday, when I was strolling with Gayle along the boardwalk in Del Mar, eating ice cream and watching the great Pacific in riffled motion, that I actually cried. We sat down on a bench beneath a rocky bluff, and I sobbed like a little boy. Embarrassed to be in tears before a fellow professional, a grown man. I put my head in my hands as he leant a solid palm to my shoulder, an encouragement.

**

We've cut and sawn for a week. The blisters on my hand have sealed over, the muscles in my arms and back taut.

I stand on the rickety porch watching toy figures paragliding in the next valley, fluorescent chutes riding the thermals. Flyers with faith in their equipment, the laws of nature. I see the first pale stars, high above the white peaks. Distance. I think about the cults I've studied, the groups of people gathered around fantastic beliefs. Comfort in the void. Whatever the fairy tale hatched to save them from the cold, they have each other.

Gayle comes out from the barn and surveys the pile of chopped brush. "I bet we cleared an acre already." He collects his notes from the table and closes the folder. "We'll have to call up for a permit to burn it though."

I follow him back inside to the kitchen. He stands in the doorway to his study, the eclectic library arranged onto walls of pine shelving. He pulls down books and reads the jacket notes. Celtic fables and Greek mythology. Psychology texts. Series of journals on forestry and fishing. Thrillers and old westerns. Each night he thumbs through them while I rinse the glasses, as if an embedded, familial routine.

"Thing is, I can't tell you half of what happens in this story." He holds a dog-eared paperback with a cowboy on the cover. "But if I turn to any page, I know the scene. The exact feeling."

He watches me slotting cutlery in the rack, nodding.

He returns the paperback and runs his finger along spines on another shelf.

I carry on with the dishes. Rainbow suds and gleaming plates. The precise heft and weight of each knife and fork, and the sudden enormity of my own presence.

"You ever read any haiku?"

"Some Basho."

He goes back to his books, but he can't find the title he's looking for. Then he realises he doesn't need it.

"When the temple bell stops ringing."

"The sound keeps coming out of the flowers."

He smiles. He takes off his baseball cap, ruffles his silver hair, and then pulls it back on. He has errands, he says, in San Diego. I dry my hands on a tea towel, and together we walk to the door where he pats my back. Like an uncle, a father.

"We'll have the break cleared by the weekend." He studies the cirrus, high above the barn. "Beautiful weather, isn't it?"

I look at the reefs of cloud. I listen to his amplified steps on the gravel drive. Wind in the sage. He gets into his station wagon, the dents and scratches, and I watch his car navigate the switchbacks down to the highway. I pick up a stone, still warm from the afternoon sun. I feel the dirt on my skin, the dust in my pores. My glorious, pounding heart, thundering in my chest.

Then Lydia's car swings through the steep turns up to the barn. Mother and daughter. The sweep of headlights across each corner, flaring on the scree. They're late, but we still have time to climb the hill and see the last glow of dusk, and I lace up my boots and step off the porch.

There are mountain lions in the rocky outcrops, muscular hunting cats with the glint of moon on their sleek pelts. As long as we hike together, the three of us will be safe.

夕焼小焼け

Yuyake, Koyake - The Going Home Song

Sunset is the end of the day,
the bell from the mountain temple rings.
Hand by hand, let's go back home with the crows.

After the children are back home,
and a full moon shines,
the birds dream, and the brightness from the stars fills the sky.

Acknowledgements

This book would not exist without the support of the following people.

First and foremost, Gill Tasker at Cargo Publishing, for taking on the manuscript and turning it from pixel to printed page. Ed Wilson, my agent at Johnson & Alcock, who had the verve and vision to forge a roughly hewn draft into a novel-shaped text. Help with my pidgin Japanese was provided by supreme linguist Jonathan Gibbard, with a more esoteric cultural education – including a research trip to Nikko – gifted by Maho Takahashi. Daniel Warriner, raconteur guide and protector in the warrens of Roppongi, must be nodded to as a muse, along with Richard Beard, who invited me into the esteemed halls of Tokyo University, and photographer Lee Chapman, whose pictures continue to inspire. David Cook, your tatami mat floor was more comfortable than I imagined. For the sight of an ocean 'like a great blue blanket pocked with feathers' I must bow to Kay Sexton. My forays into social psychology and memory were kindly analysed by Professor John Sutton of Macquarie University, and partly detailed by Salvador Murguia's study of the Pana-Wave Laboratory. Vital editing and encouragement too from Francesca Brill, Tony McGowan, and Agustina Savini, whose exemplary knowledge of the English language must exceed most native speakers.

Finally, an arigato gozaimasu to the good drivers of Japan who pulled over and picked up that straggly *gaijin* on a darkened highway. Especially the elf-like woodcutter in the wilds of Shikoku, the ancient man who mischievously dropped me at the entrance to a closed road tunnel, the path that led to Tokyo.